STRIKING

THE RESET SERIES BOOK 6

KELLEE L. GREENE

The Reset Series

Flood - Book 1

Sinking - Book 2

Drowned - Book 3

Swamp - Book 4

Torrent - Book 5

Striking - Book 6

What Remains Series

Sickness - Book 1

Outpost - Book 2

Infected - Book 3

Evasion - Book 4

Red Sky Series

Red Sky - Book 1

Blue Cloud - Book 2

Black Rain - Book 3

White Dust - Book 4

Indigo Ice - Book 5

Yellow Heat - Book 6

Ravaged Land Series (1)

Ravaged Land -Book 1

Finding Home - Book 2

Crashing Down - Book 3

Running Away - Book 4

Escaping Fear - Book 5

Fighting Back - Book 6

Ravaged Land: Divided Series (2)

The Last Disaster - Book 1

The Last Remnants - Book 2

The Last Struggle - Book 3

Ravaged Land: Eventuality Series (3)

The Wall - Book 1

The Outside - Book 2

Falling Darkness Series

Unholy - Book 1

Uprising - Book 2

Hunted - Book 3

The Island Series

The Island - Book 1

The Fight - Book 2

The Escape - Book 3

The Erased - Book 4

From Below Series

Creatures - Book 1

Desolation - Book 2

The Alien Invasion Series

The Landing - Book 1

The Aftermath - Book 2

Destined Realms Series

Destined - Book 1

JOSS

I couldn't believe that after losing both Robby and Caleb, I'd managed to continue to put one foot in front of the other for as long as I had. Months had passed since they died but the pain from losing them was just as raw as the day we had to walk away from them.

We were scared, although we didn't talk about it. It was just the three of us... Jenna, Clover, and me. And we had no idea what we were doing.

Robby told us to go south, so that's what we did. The further we could get away from the war between the two towns, the better our chances would be. Not that we had great chances at all.

I wasn't entirely sure exactly how much time had gone by since we lost them but if I had to guess, it had likely been at least two months. Maybe three. Keeping track of time wasn't easy. Days and nights blended together.

Jenna's belly was round. It was a constant reminder of what we were going to have to figure out and that time to do so was running out.

She was both worried and frightened about childbirth. What I didn't tell her was that I was absolutely terrified. I didn't know the first thing about something like that and I was sure we weren't going to just stumble into a doctor in the middle of nowhere.

The night of the war replayed over and over every time I closed my eyes. I could still hear the wailing and scream of terror of the injured and dying.

We should have done more to help them. Instead, Jenna and I ran. I told myself if we would have stayed, we would have died. It wasn't like Jenna or I could have done anything unarmed and not knowing enough to determine who were the good guys and who were the bad guys.

We were cowards. But I knew since everything happened the night the light flashed that I was a coward.

I had been part of the problem. When I'd gone with Bill, we'd gone to their land and stolen from them. I hadn't wanted to go and it hadn't been the first time but it pushed the already rolling ball harder.

There were a few moments that I'd been brave but

that was all they were—fleeting moments. I needed someone like Robby to look out for me, to watch my back, but now I didn't have anyone like him.

It was just Jenna and me. Well, and Clover too. Somehow, we were still alive even though things hadn't been easy. Honestly, though, things hadn't been easy for quite some time.

Jenna and I had managed to find an abandoned two-story house. We'd been hiding there for some time, mostly because we'd found a small stash of food. It wouldn't last and eventually, we'd have to move on.

My clothes fit looser. I always made sure Jenna had enough before taking my portion. Or I lied about how much I'd eaten. Jenna was eating for two. She needed it more than I did and I didn't have much of an appetite after what had happened to Robby and Caleb.

Sometimes it was hard to even accept that they were gone. I'd turn around, wanting to tell Caleb something but it would just be Jenna sitting there hugging herself.

"Another downpour," Jenna said at the window. She was under a heavy blanket, lightly rocking herself back and forth as she stared out at the hypnotizing rain.

"Good," I said settling down onto the sofa. I found it a bit easier to relax when the rain was falling in thick sheets.

Jenna raised a brow. "Good? Aren't you sick of the rain?"

"Of course, I am," I said. "But like I've told you before, I like to think no one would be out there traveling when it's coming down like this."

"There isn't anyone left," Jenna said.

We hadn't seen anyone since leaving the town, which, of course, was a good thing. At least I thought it was. I mean, we couldn't trust a stranger. Not again.

In the first few days, we were worried people from the town or resort were behind us... coming for us. But day after day, we were further and further, and no one came.

Most of our days since were quiet and boring. The only noise was that of our pounding hearts. I couldn't relax. I would always be looking over my shoulder and sleeping with one eye open, which was taking a toll on me.

"I'm cold," Jenna said adjusting the blanket, pulling it higher over her shoulders.

We'd figured out how to start a fire in the fireplace but it made me nervous. Not only did I worry about smoke being seen in the sky, I feared we'd run out of wood.

Being cold and bored was something we were used to but it wasn't a comfortable feeling. Jenna looked at me and frowned.

"What's wrong?" I asked.

"I have to pee again," Jenna said.

"Didn't you just do that?" I asked.

Jenna pressed her lips together. "The baby is sitting on my bladder."

"Okay, okay. Want me to come with you?" I asked.

"Thanks," she said.

Neither of us liked being alone.

I stood outside the door, crossing my arms as I waited. Every time seemed to be longer and longer but it wasn't like I had anything pressing to attend to.

"Okay," Jenna said brushing her hands over her clothing. "The buckets need to be switched out."

"I'm sure the other one is filled," I said. "Can I get you something to eat?"

I worried about Jenna not getting enough food. We'd been lucky to find vitamins in the cabinet. They were expired but I hoped that they would help to some degree. I gave her one every few days and she didn't complain.

"Pasta?" Jenna asked.

"I'd have to start a fire," I said.

"Maybe we should," Jenna said. "The baby wants something warm. I think he or she is cold."

I cocked my head to the side. "I think you're cold."

"I am," Jenna said puffing out her lip.

"Okay," I said. "Pasta with old pasta sauce it is."

"The homemade kind in the unlabeled jar or the labeled, name-brand, potentially expired one?" Jenna asked.

I exhaled slowly. "Which do you want?"

"The homemade one," Jenna said.

We walked to the kitchen together. Jenna leaned on the counter, watching as I grabbed the pot and an opened box of pasta.

"Can you get the bowls?" I asked.

"Sure," Jenna said.

There was a sound that caused her to pause. At first, I thought it was just the bowls clanking together but the look on her face made me quickly realize she hadn't made the noise.

After we'd run off from the war, Jenna had a gun. When she'd tried to shoot a small bear, we learned it was empty. Sometimes I wished we would have kept it in case we ever came across any ammo but it wouldn't have mattered. In all our travels, we hadn't found any.

Jenna reached over and grabbed a knife. She held it out in front of her.

"What is that?" I asked in a voice softer than a whisper.

She shook her head.

It sounded like someone was at the window. I set down the pasta but not the pot. When I realized it would be enough if there was an intruder, I grabbed a knife in my right hand.

Clover's feet lightly tapped the floor as she came into the kitchen to see what we were up to. I wanted to blame the sounds on the cat but when I heard the heavy clank again, I knew it hadn't come from her.

Someone was outside.

2

ADAM

It felt like everything that had happened to me since the flash of light was out of my control. I was just along for the ride.

It didn't matter what choices I made, they were always the wrong ones. All I wanted was to find a way to keep Leah safe but even that was something I constantly failed at doing.

Why she stayed with me, I couldn't even guess. Really though, what choice did she have? We hadn't seen anyone else since we'd left the resort.

Leah and I had been traveling on and off, mostly on, for months, heading in what I hoped was south. For days after we'd left, we ran. Desperate to get away from the resort as fast as we possibly could.

We hadn't stayed anywhere more than a few days

at a time. I was constantly looking over my shoulder to make sure we weren't being followed.

Even though Eva was dead, I couldn't relax. It didn't matter how far we'd gone, it never would feel as though it was far enough.

I feared we were being hunted for the deaths of Eva, the guards, and my dad. They'd want to get their revenge. There were people at the resort that followed Eva around like lovesick morons who didn't know better.

No one knew what she was capable of... the kind of person she really was. But I knew. She was dangerous... selfish. Pure evil.

The people at the resort would blame us for what had happened. Especially when they discovered we were gone. They wouldn't realize that it was Eva that was to blame.

Of course, I had no idea when the people from the resort would have returned from their war. It probably hadn't taken them more than a night to conquer the town they believed was stealing from them. What they should have done was talk to the people from the town and try to figure out a way to work together.

All of us that were left should have been working together. Instead, we were on our own. Desperately trying to find somewhere we could be safe.

"There isn't much here," Leah said shoving a few things into a backpack.

We both had a gun but even though we were armed, I still didn't feel safe. It was just a matter of time before I'd have to use it and would it be enough? Having the gun was better than nothing, so I couldn't complain.

"There isn't much left anywhere," I said. She stopped what she was doing and stared at me. I looked away. "Sorry."

She shook her head and got back to packing. "You don't have to apologize. I just don't need a reminder of how dire our situation is. Trust me, I already know."

Leah pulled the backpack over her shoulders. She walked over handing me the second pack and placed her hand on my shoulder.

"Let's get back out there," she said looking into my eyes. I could see how much she cared about me. It was a little sparkle that glimmered when our eyes connected. "We've stayed here long enough."

We'd spent two nights in the waterlogged trailer catching up on sleep. It didn't matter, though, because I was still exhausted.

The sky was light gray, the only indication that it was morning. The rain didn't stop. The clouds covered the sky, leaving us in perpetual darkness... only the shades of gray varied depending on the time of day.

The night was black—pitch black. I hated the night. The darkness, however, kept us hidden.

"Maybe we should stay another night or two," I suggested.

"We need to keep going. If we ever find a place with tons and tons of food, then we can stop for longer," Leah said walking to the living room. She tried to stuff a soft blanket into her pack but it didn't seem to fit. "Until we find the end of the rainbow, we have to keep going."

We'd been heading south for so long I figured we'd eventually hit water or maybe circle right around the earth, bringing us back to where we started. I wasn't entirely sure what we were looking for but I told myself we'd know it when we saw it.

But with every step, I lost hope we'd actually find something where we could stay. What choice did we have? We had to keep looking.

Leah and I had needed to ration food. We never had enough. I didn't mention it to her, surely, she'd noticed but Leah's hands were skin and bone.

I probably didn't look any healthier. We were slowly turning into skeletons, which was why we had to find something... somewhere... soon.

I wanted to do better for Leah. I didn't want to be a disappointment to her. Eva was right about everything she'd ever said about me. I was a failure. I was letting

Leah down. Hell, she took better care of me than I did of her.

Of course, she didn't say that. But I knew it.

"Almost ready," Leah said.

I looked around the trailer. It wasn't bad... it was small and wet but it kept us out of the rain.

A yawn widened my mouth. I tried to cover it but I wasn't fast enough.

"I wish you slept better," Leah said.

"Me too," I replied.

She crossed her arms and pressed her lips together. "Maybe we should stay another night."

"It won't matter," I sighed.

"But I thought you wanted to stay longer," Leah asked cocking a brow.

I gave her one of my best smiles. "I just hate walking in the rain."

"You could sleep. I could stay up and keep watch," Leah said. "Maybe that would help. Maybe then you could—"

"I think we should just go," I said. We needed to find more food. My tiredness and my comfort level weren't important. Getting food for Leah was what was important. "I'll sleep when we find the next place."

"Ha," Leah said dismissing my words with a wave. "You have everything?"

Leah patted her hands on herself, first checking for

the backpack, then checking for the gun. She walked over to me and helped me slide the backpack over my shoulders. Her arms wrapped around me and she kissed my cheek as her hand glided to my back.

"You're checking for my gun, aren't you?" I asked.

"What else would I be doing?" she asked grinning.

"I wouldn't say no," I said smiling back at her.

Leah rolled her eyes.

"What?" I asked innocently. "How can you not be in the mood?"

Leah blew out a breath, flinging a strand of hair into the air. She stopped at the window. "Oh, crap."

"What's wrong?" I asked feeling my stomach fill with acid.

She turned slightly but kept her eyes focused on something outside. "There's someone out there."

3

STEVIE

It wasn't a matter of if they'd come looking for us, it was a matter of when they'd come. And when they eventually did, we'd need to be ready for them.

We knew after what happened, the men from the town weren't good people. They weren't reasonable people. They wanted to control us. Take our things. Destroy us.

We did what we had to when they came. Things I didn't let myself think about.

Several months had passed since that day and I was thankful for each one but also, I knew it put us closer to the day they came looking. They'd want what we had and not just our supplies... they wanted us too.

I didn't want to find out what they would do to us. Likely some of us would die. I often wondered if they came and captured us if death would be our best-case scenario.

They'd already succeeded in killing two of the people who lived with us. It wasn't like they'd stop there. They were the type of people who would do whatever the hell they wanted if it helped them.

Jake Quinn had helped us. They'd taken his things, forcing him to stay on our property.

We focused on staying safe, and Jake helped with that by watching our surroundings. He helped us with our plan for what we'd do when the men came back. Jake was part of our team and for that, I was thankful.

The men would take everything. Then they kill us or make us do far worse things. Either way, I didn't want to find out.

Jake Quinn stayed in the house at the far end of the property. He mostly liked to be alone but also, he liked to keep watch. It was his way of helping out and because if things went south, he'd be able to easily make it to the basement.

He wasn't at the top of his game. He pretended otherwise but his medication was out and without a refill, I could tell he was worried. Jake needed to stay close to the basement because he couldn't travel far.

We'd started bringing supplies into the basement. Things that would keep us alive for weeks, hopefully, months if we got trapped down there. The basement was where we'd all go if we had to hide.

Then, of course, we'd have to hope they wouldn't find us. We still needed to work on a plan c. That was a work in progress.

The house Jake stayed in was the only one that had a basement. It was hidden in the floor and hopefully well disguised. Also, once we were all inside, Gage had built a lock on the inside he was certain would hold.

Positioned all around the property, we set up various traps and alarms. If we couldn't see them coming, we'd hear it.

Unfortunately, though, it didn't make me feel safer. There were a lot of men in the town and if they came, we would be outnumbered.

Over the last several weeks, the alarms had been triggered a few times. We were lucky that it was only more survivors. Of course, after having been so easily tricked, we had to have a much more thorough process for interviewing the newcomers.

It was an extensive process. New people were kept separate for weeks while we observed them. But the most important part was that no one was allowed to go anywhere with a new person.

Of course, it wasn't a foolproof process but it was the best we had. Trust wasn't something we could just hand out... it would need to be earned.

Our group was big and over the last few months, it had grown even more. Every time someone arrived, it was surprising that there were still people out there.

The biggest problem wasn't the rain, it was that if their group was growing, she could only assume that the group in town was also growing.

"Stevie," Ella said peeking her head into my bedroom.

"Yeah?" I said turning.

"He's back."

I smacked my hands together. "It's about damn time."

I ran down the stairs and threw my arms around Gage who was soaking wet. He squeezed me back.

"Hey, pal," he said.

"I was starting to get worried," I said.

He pulled back and grinned. "Only first starting to worry now?"

"I know you can take care of yourself," I said. I stood back and crossed my arms. "Did you find anything?"

"No," he said looking away. "I tried, though, Stevie. Everything is just... it's gone."

Gage had traveled further south in the hopes of finding somewhere else we could escape to should we need it. A few weeks ago, he'd traveled west, which hadn't turned up much either.

Everything was flooded... washed away... destroyed.

We couldn't go east and we couldn't go south. West was out too. The only two choices we had were to protect what we had or go north and fight.

When I looked into Gage's eyes, I saw that he knew it too. At some point, we'd have to tell the others.

"Where's Shawn?" Gage asked.

I shrugged. "I think he's working on the basement. He was gone before I woke up."

"Good," Gage said. "Everyone knows about the basement, right?"

"Yes," I said. I lowered my voice so those in the kitchen wouldn't hear me. "But it's going to be hard to get everyone down there if they come."

"We'll do some trial runs," Gage said.

I let out a breath. "Even with practice, I'm not sure we'll all get down there. And if we do, we won't be able to stay down there forever."

"Maybe they won't stick around," Gage said.

"Or maybe they'll all move here," I said.

"We'll have to refine our plan," Gage said.

I rubbed my forehead, trying to erase the growing tension. Gage placed his hand on my shoulder.

"We'll figure it out," he said. "Not to mention we're growing. Maybe we can take them. Give us a little credit."

"I need to keep everyone safe," I said. "That's my only job. I couldn't ever ask anyone to risk their lives."

"Did you ever think that maybe it's this place that's worth fighting for?" Gage asked.

The front door opened with an intrusive squeak. Shawn's eyes were wide. He didn't acknowledge Gage.

Something was wrong.

Shawn sucked in a quick breath. "We have a problem."

4

JOSS

Jenna walked over to me. Our shoulders touched as we took small steps toward the living room, which was where I thought the sounds had come from.

The clanking and scratching noises had stopped. It no longer sounded as though someone was trying to come in through the window.

We stood there in silence for several minutes.

"Did we imagine that?" Jenna asked squeezing my arm with her fingertips.

"Maybe it was Clover," I said.

"You know as well as I do that it wasn't Clover making those noises," Jenna said.

Jenna looked at me with wide eyes. "What will we do if someone is out there?"

"Hope they leave," I said.

"What if they get inside?"

"There's nothing here. They won't stay," I said.

Jenna blinked. "Except for us."

"No one would want us," I said flatly.

"Don't kid yourself," Jenna said. "They'll have their way with us and then turn us into a meal."

"Gross," I said handing Jenna my knife as I slowly continued toward the front window.

My palm lightly rested on the cool wall as I leaned forward. I curled my finger around the curtain and started to pull it back, stopping abruptly when a shadow moved past the window.

I swallowed down a breath as Jenna pulled me back. My heart pounded so loudly I worried whoever was outside could hear it.

"Here," Jenna whispered giving me the knife back. "You might still need this."

I jumped back at the scratching sound next to the window. It was like something was pawing at the siding of the house... nothing like what I'd imagine it would sound like if a person was trying to get inside.

I sucked in a breath and moved back to the window. My fingers stiffened. I shook my hands and hooked my finger behind the curtain.

I moved slower than a turtle as I pulled it back, stopping when I saw the black fur. My shoulders relaxed and I jerked the curtain halfway open to reveal our visitor to Jenna.

"Wonder if it's the same one we saw miles back," I said.

Jenna exhaled. "That was weeks ago."

"Was it?" I asked shaking my head. "Still, it could be the same one. Maybe it followed us."

"It would have made a meal of us," Jenna said. "Poor thing is so thin. We should try to catch it."

"We have enough pets to feed," I said.

Jenna rolled her eyes. "Funny."

"There isn't much left on its bones."

"But there is some," Jenna said looking as though she was staring at a table with an entire Thanksgiving dinner perched upon it.

"Maybe we should try to catch whatever it's been eating," I suggested. "Squirrels, rabbits... whatever."

"We don't know the first thing about setting a trap," Jenna said with a frown.

I shrugged. "Guess we'll just have to figure it out."

"I think killing the bear might be easier," Jenna said.

"It's too dangerous," I said. "All we have is knives."

Jenna raised a brow. "And that pot."

"I can't bash it over the head, can you?" I asked.

"Maybe," Jenna said.

"No," I said shaking my head. "You or I could get

seriously hurt or even killed. We have no idea what that thing is capable of, even in its current condition."

Jenna held up her hand. "Maybe we could find some ropes. We could figure out a way to tie it up."

"Let's say we managed that. You're going to slit its throat?" I asked.

"I will," Jenna said confidently.

My eyes quickly shifted away from her. "Well, we don't have any rope. And it would probably try to bite you if you get close to it."

"That's where the pot comes in, I guess," Jenna said as if it all made sense to her. "Knock it out."

"I don't think you know me at all," I said.

"I think you have to change who you are," Jenna said.

I sighed. She wasn't wrong. "Fine. Let's find some rope."

"You're serious?" she asked.

"Yeah, I guess. But we have to wait until it's safe."

It wasn't like we were going to catch it anyway. There was no reason we couldn't try to set up traps for smaller animals. Maybe we could catch a squirrel or something, not that I would have any idea how to cook it.

The house we were staying in had a garage that wasn't attached to the house. There was also a shed in the back but we'd have to wait until the bear was going before venturing out.

He didn't stick around long. When he hadn't been able to get the food, he moved on.

"It's gone," Jenna said staring out of the window. "Let's set up."

"This is never going to work," I said.

"There's the negative Nancy I know and love," Jenna said.

I raised a brow. "Love, huh?"

"Yeah, sure, why not?" Jenna's brow wrinkled. "You mean, you don't feel the same."

I blinked repeatedly.

She punched me in the shoulder. "Relax. We are all that's left, though."

"Yeah," I murmured as we walked out of the house toward the garage.

We found a long rope, which we tied into a large loop and tossed one end over a branch. The branch's strength was questionable but there wasn't a great chance the bear would come back.

We'd also found several large bins that we set up with a thin branch. I tied a piece of twine to the bottom of the twig and at the backside, I placed a chunk of beef jerky.

"Now, all we do is wait," Jenna said. She blew out a puff of air. "In the rain."

"We have more twine," I said turning toward the house. "Maybe we can't put the string through the window or under the door."

"That's not a bad idea," Jenna said. "Although I'm not sure it'll work."

We tried a couple different methods. It didn't work through the window because we were unable to lock the window with the twine underneath. And under the door didn't work because it was pinched too tightly, making it impossible to pull on the string.

The only way that would work would be to sit outside in the rain. I let out a breath.

"I guess we'll take turns sitting in the rain," I said.

"I guess so," Jenna said crossing her arms. She turned slowly, meeting my eyes. "Or we could both sit out here together."

I forced a smile. "Okay. Sure. For a while, anyway."

It wasn't even twenty minutes before Jenna gave up. The bear didn't come back and there were no signs of other wildlife.

It was sad but I'd known we wouldn't catch anything. I followed her back inside.

We gathered up our supplies for pasta and got to work on making food. The fire was warm and perfect. I stared into the flames as the food heated. My thoughts drifted and I didn't realize I was thinking about Robby until a tear rolled down my cheek.

I quickly wiped it away and portioned out the food. A huge pile for Jenna and what would be just enough for me.

It wasn't until after we'd finished and I brought everything in the kitchen to clean up that I decided to check the cabinets. Our food situation was edging on dire.

I had no idea how long we had until we'd have to leave to find a new place... more food... more supplies. Jenna and traveling weren't a good mix. It had caused her pain, although she'd tried to hide it ever since we'd lost Robby and Caleb.

I'd wait to tell Jenna... until I had a better idea of when we'd have to leave. Maybe it would just be me that would leave. Could I do that? Would she even want me to do that?

Maybe I wouldn't have a choice.

5

ADAM

The young woman had her hands at her sides, balled up into tight fists. There was a big, brown satchel over her shoulder but otherwise, she had nothing. She seemed to be wandering from side to side but mostly, she moved forward toward the trailer.

She was bone thin. Worse off than we were. And she looked frightened. Worse than we did.

Her skin was pale and her long, wet hair dirty and stringy. She needed help.

"I don't think we need to worry about her," I said.

"Never let your guard down," Leah said.

"You're right," I said turning to her. "So, what are we going to do?"

Leah met my gaze for a second. "We're going to help her as best as we can but we aren't going to let our guard down."

"This isn't going to help with my sleeping issues," I said.

"We'll make it quick. Give her some food and water. Then we'll see if she knows anything." Leah straightened her spine. "Then we'll be on our way."

I nodded. Even though the girl was thin and frightened, I was still nervous. Over my travels, it felt as though more people were bad than they were good.

Someone could easily say the same thing about me. I'd killed. My excuse was that I was doing it to help... for survival but my life wasn't more important than anyone else.

Shit.

There was a time I thought I had everything figured out, well, except for my love life. I'd know who I was but now I had no idea.

"Ready?" Leah asked.

"Yeah," I said.

Leah gestured toward my back. "Take out your gun."

"Seriously?"

"Yes," Leah said. "Just in case."

"I... I don't want to scare her," I said.

Leah let out a breath. "Fine." She took out her gun. "Perhaps it'll be less scary for her if I'm the one holding it."

It wasn't exactly what I'd meant but I didn't feel

like getting in an argument over it when the girl was almost to the trailer. Leah took my hand and pulled me out of the front door.

The girl stopped abruptly. She held out her hands but then her lips curled into a smile.

"Hello!" she chirped.

Leah and I exchanged a look. It was a greeting we hadn't been expecting.

"I'm so happy to see people," she said. "Say, I know this is incredibly weird but can I have a hug?"

I shook my head. Leah's brow wrinkled.

"Oh." Her body deflated slightly. "I told you it was weird. Maybe another time. It's just been so long."

The girl wasn't old. She was maybe sixteen or seventeen. It was amazing she was surviving on her own. I wasn't even sure I would have been able to accomplish something like that. I needed Leah at my side.

"How long?" Leah asked.

"A few weeks, I think," she said.

"What's your name?" Leah asked.

The girl smiled. "Heather, and you?"

"Leah. This is Adam."

"My parents were murdered," Heather blurted out. She gasped and slapped her hand over her mouth. "I can't believe I just said that."

"Are you okay?" Leah asked.

Heather shrugged. "Physically? Yeah. Mentally? I've been better. I wasn't in the house when the men came. I don't know what happened but I heard the gunshots. I stayed hidden... I waited in a thorny shrub through the night until the men left. I was a coward. I should have done something more."

"That's awful," Leah said slowly approaching the girl. She held out her arms and the girl leaped into her arms. "I'm so sorry."

"I went into the house," Heather said. "I shouldn't have gone back inside. I knew it was too late to do anything."

Leah gave her a quick squeeze before stepping back. "Let's go inside. I'll give you something to eat and drink."

"Really?" Heather asked.

"Yeah, of course," Leah said.

I followed them back inside the trailer. Heather sat down at the table and Leah gave her a bottle of water.

"Did you ever see those men again?" Leah asked.

"No, thank God," Heather said. "I wish I could ask them why, though. My parents were good people. They would have shared anything we had with them. They didn't need to kill them."

"People do crazy stuff," I said.

Heather's head bobbed. "My parents and I were going to eventually make our way to my uncle's place."

"Why?" Leah asked.

"He has a place in New Mexico. I'd only visited a few times but he was always wanted to show us what he was building," Heather said.

My eyes narrowed. "What was he building?"

"Long before all this happened, he was working on one of those bunker things. He'd send pictures and links to my dad of all the things he was doing." Heather chuckled softly. "My uncle was always trying to convince my parents to do the same."

Leah's eyes brightened. "That's where you're going? To your uncles?"

"I'm trying but I can't say I'm doing a very good job," Heather said.

"You said you've only been there a few times?" I asked.

"That's right," Heather said. "Which is partly why I'm doing such a bad job. When I get closer, I'm sure I'll be able to find it." Heather clasped her hands together. "Is this New Mexico?"

I shook my head. "I'm not sure. It might be Colorado."

"But it could be New Mexico?" Heather asked.

"Could be," I said. "Everything kind of all looks the same now."

"It sure does." Heather frowned.

Heather started crying. She hugged herself while her shoulders bobbed.

Leah looked at me as if she wanted me to do or say something. I was almost sure there wasn't anything I could say that was comforting.

"There, there," I said awkwardly patting the top of her head.

Leah sighed.

"I'm not going to make it on my own," Heather said. "I barely even made it this far. Where are you two going?"

I opened my mouth but Leah spoke before I could squeeze out a word.

"We're just looking for somewhere safe," Leah said.

"You guys aren't going to kill me, are you?" Heather asked.

Leah narrowed her eyes. "Why would we do that?"

"I don't know," Heather said covering a small giggle. "I haven't slept in a couple days. You have to forgive me. But if you are going to kill me, would you please get it over with?"

"We're not going to kill you," Leah said both trying to sound reassuring while the question seemingly irritated her.

"Okay," Heather said sucking in a breath that made her bottom lip quiver. "Good. Can I come with you then? I promise I won't be any trouble."

Leah sat down next to her and placed her hand over Heather's. "We don't know where we're going. We've had our own struggles and prefer to go on our own way."

There was a long pause. Heather sobbed but she nodded.

"I understand," Heather said.

"I'm sorry," Leah said.

"No, it's fine. I shouldn't have asked," Heather said. "Still, it was very nice to talk to actual people. Unless, of course, I'm dreaming all of this. Either way, it's still nice."

Leah stood. She pulled some food out of her backpack and set it on the table.

"We should go," Leah said meeting my eyes. "I hope you find your uncle."

"Good luck," I said wanting to roll my eyes at myself.

I didn't feel great about leaving the girl. Maybe we should have tried to help her, although I didn't know how we'd be able to do that when we were barely able to take care of ourselves.

I gave her a little wave before stepping outside into the rain. She smiled and waved back.

"Are we doing the right thing?" I asked after we'd walked in silence for at least a mile. I glanced back but

I couldn't see the trailer... just a few trees and dead shrubs scattered about in the mud.

"I hope so," Leah said. "But I can't stop thinking about her."

"Me too," I said. "We could go back."

Leah glanced over her shoulder. Her lips pressed together.

"We don't need to," she said.

"What do you mean?"

Leah raised a brow. "She's about a quarter of a mile back. Running from tree to tree. She's been following us since we left."

6

STEVIE

The rain poured down on us. Thunder rumbled in the distance to our west.

I stood there with my arms folded as I stared at the house. My lips allowed a slow breath to escape.

"How did this happen?" I asked staring at the hole in the roof.

The only bright side was that it happened to the smallest house on the property. If it had happened to the main house, it would have disrupted our daily life.

It was one of the buildings we used for storage but that hadn't meant that no one had been inside.

I looked at Shawn and then around the area. "No one got hurt, right?"

"Stevie, seriously." Shawn raised a single brow. "If someone had been hurt, don't you think I would have started with that?"

"Probably," I said running my palms down the back of my soaked hair. "Dammit. We need to get everything out of there before the whole thing collapses."

"I'll gather the others," Shawn said.

Ever since the men from the town had come to our home, I was anxious anytime we were outside for too long. Not just for myself but for everyone who lived at the compound.

"Not too many," I called after him.

We needed to work quickly to salvage whatever we could but too many people could slow us down. Not to mention, it felt like it would put too many of the others in danger.

"That doesn't look fixable," Gage said.

"No, no, it doesn't," I replied.

"Doesn't mean I won't try," Gage said pulling in a breath that shook his arms.

I twisted my fingers together. "Of course, it doesn't. But first things first. How can we prevent this from happening to the other buildings?"

"I'm not sure," Gage said. "It's not like the weight of the water caused this, I think it's because it's just too waterlogged. There isn't anything we can do besides praying for the rain to stop."

"If praying stopped the rain, it wouldn't be raining anymore," I said.

Shawn was already on his way back with five others. Ella and Noah looked concerned.

"We kept all the good stuff in here," Noah said as he approached. I noticed that Shawn and Noah were holding the shotguns.

"Two stand guard while the others work. We'll all take turns," Shawn said.

I offered an approving nod. "Good thinking."

"Where do you want us to put all this stuff?" Shawn asked.

"Some in the basement, I guess. Some in the main house and...." A frustrated sigh escaped from between my pursed lips. "We'll just have to put it wherever we can find space."

Gage pressed his lips together and pointed at the two houses closest to the one Jack Quinn stayed in. "Those two have room upstairs and on the first floor too."

"Let's start there then," I said.

The water dripped down inside the house. It didn't fall in little drops, it poured in like it was coming from a filthy, broken faucet.

I worried about climbing the drenched carpeted stairs. The last thing we needed was someone getting hurt if the stairs collapsed.

"They seem sturdy enough," Gage said hopping a bit on each step while holding onto the banister.

"It's like you read my mind," I said.

"We've been together for quite some time now, Stevie," Gage said with a smile. "I can read your expressions."

I cocked my head slightly. "So, we don't have to talk?"

"Should I be offended by that comment?" Gage asked with a laugh. His playful mood instantly vanished when he reached the second floor. Gage looked up, placing his hands on his hips. "Well, shit."

I wasn't an expert in anything but I knew the roof was unfixable. "Wow. Now I'm worried about the other houses."

"Let's hope this was due to faulty construction," Gage said shaking his head. "I don't know but we should work fast."

"Agreed," I said.

We moved the stuff to the closest house first. It didn't take us as long as I had expected.

"Let's get these last boxes over to Jake's house," I called.

I led the way. Shawn and Gage held the shotguns as they escorted us down the road.

My eyes scanned the horizon. I couldn't see far because of the mist the rain created. I kept blinking, afraid I was seeing shadows of people watching us in the distance.

"Everything okay?" Shawn asked.

"I thought I saw something," I said.

"Where?" he asked adjusting his grip on the gun.

I waved my hand in the air. "It was my imagination."

"Are you sure?"

"Yeah. I think so," I said.

"That doesn't reassure me."

I turned, looking at the horizon again. "It's just rain."

"Could be animals," Shawn said.

I shook my head. "It's nothing. Relax."

"You're telling me to relax?" Shawn asked with a soft chuckle.

I rested the box against the door frame. I raised my hand and knocked on the door.

My eyes shifted back toward the horizon and Shawn followed my gaze. He opened his mouth but I spoke before he could say anything.

"It's just rain and shadows, okay?"

I knocked again. It felt as though we'd been standing there for a long time. The others shifted their weight impatiently while holding the heavy boxes. It was odd that Jake hadn't answered the door.

"Maybe he's using the bathroom," Gage said.

"Jake?" I called as I knocked again.

He didn't come to the door. I shook my head as a heavy worry filled my stomach.

"Do you have a key?" Noah asked setting down the box he was holding.

"I have it," Shawn said stepping forward. He unlocked the door and stuck his head inside. "Jake? Are you here?"

Every once in a while, he walked over to the main house for one of Kieran's warm meals. He ate quickly and he never stayed long but he enjoyed her cooking.

No answer.

I pushed past Shawn and entered the room. I set the box down and moved through the house nervously.

"Jake!" I called as I headed from room to room. "Where are you?"

My heart pounded harshly. It felt like I was being stabbed with razor blades on the inside.

I passed the partially opened bedroom door and stopped. Something had caught my eye.

A pair of boots, Jake's boots, pointed up toward the ceiling. I pushed open the door.

He was lying on the floor... not moving. "Jake!"

7

JOSS

It wasn't more than a few days before I broke down and told Jenna. I couldn't keep it a secret when she'd asked about why I hadn't made more of my infamous watered-down oatmeal.

"We'll just ration," Jenna said. "I'll be okay."

I paced the floor. "No, we can't do that. You're pregnant. You need it."

"You've been giving me too much the way it is," Jenna said shifting on the sofa to get into a more comfortable position. "There's still a chance the bear will come back."

I groaned. "That bear isn't going to come back. It's probably out there dead somewhere."

Jenna stood, stomping her way to the kitchen. I followed her, watching as she pulled open every cabinet.

"Look," Jenna said holding out her arms to each side. "We have plenty. You're overreacting."

"I'm not overreacting," I said my eyes shifted toward her belly. It somehow looked even bigger today, which was a good sign. It meant the baby was still growing.

Jenna waved her hands. "You really are. We have week's worth of food left."

"You're kidding, right?" I asked shaking my head.

"Not even a little," Jenna said. Her eyes widened. "And I still have hope that bear will come back."

I exhaled as my eyes rolled.

"Let's go sit outside a while," Jenna said.

"Jenna," I groaned. I hated getting wet. We didn't have a large selection of clothing to choose from. The owners of the house we were in hadn't left much behind and what they had left didn't fit particularly well.

Whenever we went outside, we'd have to undress and wear something ill-fitting until our clothing dried. It was uncomfortable, not to mention it made me nervous to not be in my own clothes. If someone came... or if something happened... well, I wanted to be in my usual outfit.

"Okay," I said.

We went outside and hid under a blue tarp at the

side of the house. The second I sat down, my pants were soaked. Mud seeped in, staining the fabric.

"I kind of miss the store," Jenna said. "All those clean clothes. I could wear something new every day."

It was the first time she brought up something from when the guys were alive. My stomach swirled. It suddenly tasted like I'd swallowed an entire lemon wedge.

Jenna turned to me. "What do you think happened to it? Do you think it's gone? Flooded?"

"Probably," I said. I didn't want to talk about the store. It brought back all the memories of Caleb and Robby. Good memories. Something really close to happy memories.

At the time, I hadn't felt entirely safe but it had been the closest I'd come... since after everything. I desperately wanted to change the subject but couldn't think of a damn thing to change it to.

"I slept so much better at the store," Jenna said. "And it would have been a much cleaner and safer place to have a baby."

"The store is gone," I said sharply.

Jenna hesitated. "I know that duh. Sorry for wishing things weren't so shitty."

"They could be worse," I said getting to my feet. "I need a break. We're not going to catch anything in this rain."

"You're leaving me?" Jenna said.

"I'm going inside," I said.

Jenna sighed. I felt bad but I couldn't do it. I couldn't reminisce. It would only remind me of everything I'd lost.

She followed me inside. We didn't talk the rest of the night except for when Jenna needed to use the bathroom.

We went upstairs to sleep, locking ourselves in a bedroom like we did most nights. It didn't take Jenna long to fall asleep but I sat there staring at the window for what felt like hours.

My eyes abruptly popped open at the sounds coming from downstairs. Jenna must have gotten up to get something to eat. She didn't want me to know.

I started to roll over but my body stopped when I rolled into Jenna. My eyes widened. The noises were real and I most definitely wasn't asleep.

"Jenna," I whispered as I lightly shook her body.

"Shh," she said pulling the blanket over her shoulder.

"Did you forget to lock the door when you came in?" I asked.

She must have heard the sounds. Fear saturated her face.

"Of course, I did," Jenna whispered. "Must be Clover."

Clover was curled up at the bottom of the bed near my feet. She didn't seem to care about the noises one bit.

"It's not Clover," I said.

"The bear?" Jenna asked.

I shrugged but it seemed unlikely. "It sounds like someone in the kitchen. Are you sure you locked the door when you came in?"

"I didn't come in last. You did."

"No," I said shaking my head. "It was you."

"Well, then, I'm sure I locked it," Jenna said.

I grabbed the knife from the nightstand but I didn't get off the bed. I didn't want to make even the slightest of noises.

"What are we going to do?" Jenna asked mostly hissing the question.

"I guess we'll wait until they leave," I said.

"What if they don't leave?" Jenna asked. "What if it's the bear?"

We fell silent at the distant sound of someone using the bathroom. I slowly turned to Jenna.

"It's not the bear," I said.

A cabinet closed in the kitchen. Seconds later, creaking sounds of another opening.

"They're taking our food, Joss. We need that food." Jenna sighed. "We have to do something."

I waved my hand frantically while I silently shushed her. My fingers squeezed the knife handle.

Slowly, I swung my legs over the side of the bed. I slipped my feet into my still soaked shoes, hoping the squishing was only something I would hear.

"Put your shoes on," I said over my shoulder.

"Why?" Jenna asked.

My mouth was as dry as a desert. I winced as I swallowed hard.

"In case we have to run," I said.

Jenna repeatedly nodded as she put on her shoes. There wasn't much light in the room but there was enough from the candle to show me the fear on her face.

She held onto my arm as we moved toward the staircase. We didn't make a sound. We also only made it halfway down the stairs when we had stop.

My hand was shaking. My muscles were frozen in place.

There was a girl, not much younger than I was, sitting on the sofa. She had no idea we were there as she stuck her fingers in the peanut butter jar. Our peanut butter jar.

I finished my descent, holding the knife out in front of me. It wasn't until I reached the last step the girl looked up and screamed.

"Shh!" I said worried someone might hear her.

The girl dropped the peanut butter jar on the floor. Her eyes locked on the table near the front door. A gun.

Jenna had moved fast but not as fast as the girl. She picked up the weapon and held it up in her shaking hand.

"Don't shoot!" I said holding up my hands without dropping the knife.

Jenna's hand shot forward and she quickly disarmed the girl. She took a step back and aimed it at her.

"That was our peanut butter," Jenna said.

"I'm sorry," the girl said. "I didn't know anyone was here. Please don't kill me."

Jenna's anger was apparent in her unblinking eyes. "You can't just go into a house and steal people's food."

"I'm sorry," the girl repeated. "I'm so hungry."

"Get out of our house," Jenna shouted. Her arms were stiff and there was no trembling in her hands.

The girl covered her face and whimpered. Suddenly she dropped her hands and took a quick step forward.

"Fine," the girl said. "Kill me. Go on then. Get it over with. I can't do this anymore." She dropped to her knees. "I just can't do this anymore!"

8

ADAM

Heather cheered when we stopped and waved her over. She hugged us both repeatedly.

"Thank you so much," she said reaching out to me again.

I smiled and held up my hand to stop her. "Whoa, okay, okay. You're welcome."

She clasped her hands to her chest and hesitated. The second I lowered my hand, she lunged forward and hugged me again.

"Sorry. I can't help it. I'm just so happy and thankful," Heather said. "It's quite possible you two have saved my life."

"It seems as though you forgot we left you behind," I said.

Leah shot me a look so sharp it felt it stab the

center of my chest. I winced and Leah shifted her eyes forward.

"It's okay," Heather said. "I get it. You don't know me or anything about me but I'm a good person. You'll see."

We'd walked for miles without talking. The rain falling and plopping into the mud was hypnotizing.

I was tired. We were all tired but we pushed forward toward a beat-up gas station, or at least what remained of it, in the distance.

The ground was slick. My foot slipped slightly and I flopped my arms around to regain my balance.

Heather covered her laugh. Leah didn't bother.

"Mud skating?" Leah asked shaking her head.

She took two steps before her foot skidded and slipped out from under her. Leah fell heavily to the ground.

"That's what you get for laughing," I said crouching down next to her.

Her brow wrinkled as her hand stretched forward to the side of her leg. She rubbed her hand back and forth.

"Ow," she said with a painful grimace.

"Are you okay?" I asked.

Leah shook her head and rolled up the leg of her pants. "I think I'm bleeding."

She started shaking her hands. I looked down and noticed a rusty piece of metal sticking out of the mud.

"Oh, oh, oh," Leah said sucking in quick breaths. "It burns."

Blood was gushing out of the cut and into the mud. I leaned in closer. With the amount of blood coming out of the wound, it was hard to tell exactly how bad it was but I could see it wasn't good.

"Let me take a look," Heather said kneeling down beside me. She placed her bag in the mud and pulled open the flap.

My eyes flicked to the side, unable to stop myself from glancing into her bag. She had bottles of medicine, gauze, and all sorts of medical supplies. A small pharmacy all in one place.

Heather splashed on some liquid before quickly placing a thick strip of gauze over the wound. She wrapped tape around it and frowned. Her eyes met mine for a quick second before she quickly closed the bag.

"I'm sorry," Heather said. "I'll do a better job once we get inside. Can you stand?"

"I think so," Leah said. The muscles in her neck popped out as she clenched her jaw. "Hurts like a... like a lot."

Heather reached into her bag and pulled out a

white bottle. She twisted the cap off and took out two orange pills.

"Take these," Heather said.

"I'm not really sure I should just take pills from strangers," Leah said.

Heather raised the bottle. "Pain pills. Name brand."

"Well, you could have just put them in that bottle," Leah said.

Heather shrugged. "Would you feel more comfortable if I took some too? Seems wasteful, though."

"It wouldn't help," Leah said.

"Okay," Heather said holding out the bottle. "Put them back then."

"Never mind," Leah said. She looked at me and cocked a brow. "Wish me luck."

Leah popped the pills in her mouth before I could say anything. Hopefully, whatever Heather had given her really was pain medicine.

Heather and I helped Leah traverse the slippery mud. It wasn't easy but we made it to the gas station.

"Wait out here," I said taking out my gun.

"What are you doing?" Leah asked.

"Making sure it's safe," I said.

Leah sighed. "And if it's not, what are we going to do? I can't run away. If someone is in there, we're screwed either way."

"That's depressing," Heather said puffing out her lower lip.

Leah took out her gun. "Let's go in."

It didn't take long to check the small, stinky gas station. No one had been around in a while. There was dust on the shelves that still held a few items.

"Pack up what we can," Leah said sitting down on the floor. She placed her hand on her leg. "Why do I smell hot dogs?"

On the counter near the register was an old hot dog warmer. Thankfully, it was empty.

The front of the gas station was a large, cracked glass window. Anyone passing by would have been able to see us inside. There was a bathroom and a back office, which we decided to hide in while Heather took another look at Leah's leg.

"Why do you have all that medicine?" I asked as I sat down in the squeaky office chair behind the desk.

Heather shrugged. "My mom was a nurse. I had a bag with food but that's gone now. My uncle probably has more medicine, which we might need. I don't know much but we want to make sure your cut doesn't get infected. I wish I knew how to stitch you up."

"You think I need stitches?" Leah asked blinking slowly.

"Probably," Heather said with several quick nods.

"We're lucky you followed us," I said.

Leah's head bobbed. "Really lucky. Things could have been much worse. I don't think we have anything other than maybe a couple bandages I was able to get from the resort. I can't believe I was so careless."

"That piece of metal blended right in with the mud," I said. "There wasn't anything you could have done differently."

"Really?" Leah asked sharply. "You and Heather didn't slice open your legs."

I looked down.

"Sorry," Leah said. "I'm mad at myself. Not you. I just don't know what we're going to do. We can't stay here long. That big window makes me nervous."

I crossed my arms and leaned back in the chair. It squealed like a baby pig being pulled from its mother when I tipped too far back. I waved my arms wildly as I leaned forward to stop myself from tipping.

They both ignored my clumsiness. I cleared my throat, pretending I hadn't just nearly fell over.

"Only one door in and out too," I said.

"Right," Leah said sighing as she pulled the bottom of her pant leg up to her knee. Blood had already soaked through the gauze. "Dammit."

"We should go to my uncle's place," Heather said. "He could probably help you. Better than I can for sure."

Leah frowned. "What if I can't make it that far?"

My stomach twisted. Leah was tough. If she was questioning her ability to continue, well, then things were worse than she was letting on.

"No one knows about the place," Heather said. "If we can make it there, we'll be safe."

I looked into Leah's eyes. "What do you think?"

She looked down at her leg and then back at me. I thought she was going to give me the answer but she just shook her head.

We never thought we'd be with anyone else again, yet here we were with Heather. And not only that but Heather wanted us to go join her uncle.

How could we trust her? After everything we'd gone through, how could we trust anyone?

Heather could have kept what was in her bag a secret. She didn't have to help Leah but she did.

"I should change your bandage," Heather said.

Leah nodded.

I watched as Heather carefully removed the gauze, applied an antibiotic foam, and then wrapped her up again. She was careful. Delicate.

"You're really good at that," I said.

"My mom was a good teacher. She wanted me to be a nurse too," Heather said closing up her bag. "It was my parent's plan for me but then this all happened. My mom helped people after everything. My dad too. They were good people. I miss them."

"Sorry," I said. "I miss my parents too."

Heather quickly wiped away a tear. "I don't like to think about it too much. It's easier when I don't."

"I get it," I said.

I could relate. Of course, I didn't bother to tell Heather that my father was murdered in front of me. The feelings were still probably very similar.

"We should go," Leah said getting to her feet. "I don't like it here. We need to find somewhere else and put in a few more miles."

"A few more miles?" I looked down at her leg. "Are you sure?"

"I'm sure as hell going to try." Leah smiled. "Hell, if I'm going to let a little scratch stop me."

We didn't walk for long before we came upon a small shed. There were a few hours before it would be too dark to walk but we stopped anyway. I could tell Leah was struggling but I yawned and said I needed to rest.

It wasn't a lie. I did need to sleep. But stopping in the shed wasn't going to help me get any sleep. I wasn't sure if anything ever would.

During the night, Leah was resting on my shoulder. Her entire body vibrated against mine.

"Are you okay?" I asked.

Leah's teeth chattered. "I'm so cold."

9

STEVIE

I dropped down to my knees and put my hands on his chest. I had no idea what I was doing but I kept touching his warm body.

Gage leaped over his legs and was on the other side in seconds. He lightly shook his body. "Mr. Quinn... Jake. Are you okay?"

He took his limp hand and held it, his fingertips moving around his wrist.

"He has a pulse," Gage said.

"I'll get Kieran," Shawn said.

His loud footsteps echoed as he ran through the house. I lightly tapped my palm to Jake's cheek.

"Wake up, Jake," I begged. "Please, wake up."

The man's eyelids fluttered. He groaned as he tried to open them but they barely budged.

"Jake!" I said. "Hey, we're here, okay?"

"I'll get him some water," Gage said hopping over him again.

"What happened?" I asked keeping my hand on Jake's shoulder.

Jake tried to speak but he couldn't find his voice. Gage returned with the water and we helped him take a small drink.

Kieran came into the room with Shawn behind her. She was soaked and out of breath.

"Oh, Mr. Quinn," she said taking his hand into hers. "What happened?"

Jake cleared his throat. "Let me get up."

There was no way he'd be able to get to his feet on his own. Of course, Jake Quinn wasn't the type of guy that would ask for help.

Kieran and I helped him to the bed. He laid down and gripped his chest. Jake controlled his breathing.

"Oh, Mr. Quinn," Kieran said with worry stretching her face. "Please, tell me what happened."

"It's my damn heart," Jake said. "I need my medicine."

I looked down at my feet.

"Every day has been getting harder," Jake said.

"Why didn't you tell me?" Kieran asked.

Jake grinned. "Oh, I wasn't going to bother you with my nonsense."

"Your heart issue isn't nonsense," Kieran said. "Is that all that's been bothering you?"

"I've been retaining water. My legs are swelling," Jake said. "My pulse is low but none of it really bothers me. Just takes me by surprise if I get up too fast."

"I'll see if I can find anything that might help with those things," Kieran said squeezing his hand. "Can I get you anything else?"

Jake's eyes brightened. "I like that flatbread you make."

"I might have some left," Kieran said as she stood and made her way to the door. She stopped, flashing a smile over her shoulder. "And if I don't, I'll make a special batch just for you."

Jake's cheeks reddened a pinch. He cleared his throat and put his normal scowl back on before anyone else noticed.

Shawn met my eyes before leaving the room. It was his way of letting me know that he'd be escorting Kieran back to our house.

"You're all making me nervous hovering around like pesky mosquitos." Jake waved his left hand in the air. "Go on about your business."

"We're just worried about you," I said.

"No one needs to worry about me," Jake said.

I touched the back of his hand before jerking my

chin toward the door. Everyone scuttled out of the room.

"I'm going to have someone sitting at your window whether you like it or not," I said quickly holding up my hand so he couldn't argue. "Just until you're back on your feet."

"I'll be good again in no time," Jake said.

"I know you will," I said. "Until then, someone will be at the window."

I didn't bother to tell him I was going to check on him as often as I could. It would just make him angry.

On the way back to the house, I thought about how badly Jake needed his medicine. Hell, he probably needed to be seen by an actual doctor but that obviously wasn't an option.

Kieran stepped out of the front door when she saw me. "Stevie, I'm going to stay with Jake."

"I'm not super comfortable with that," I said noticing the small bag over her shoulder. "And what about Lucy? We need you here."

"I'll come back often," Kieran said. "But someone needs to be there with him... just in case. We'll sleep in the basement. There's a sofa down there and I'll sleep on the cot."

I opened my mouth but she held up a finger.

"Don't argue. I've already spoken with Lucy about it," Kieran said.

It wasn't like she had much time to talk with Lucy. She probably told Lucy what the situation would be. There likely wasn't any discussion on the matter, much like she wasn't allowing me to have.

"We'll be safer that way," Kieran said.

"What if something does happen?" I asked crossing my arms.

Kieran cocked her head to the side. "I'll do the best I can to help him. He's a good man, Stevie and we all need more men like him."

I couldn't argue with her. Jake Quinn was on the grumpy side but he was easily a good guy. He would have done anything to help us. In fact, he had tried, and he barely even knew us.

"I'll be back to make all the meals," Kieran said. "Staying with him won't get in the way of my duties."

"Are you sure about this?"

"I'm doing it whether or not you like it or he likes it," Kieran said. "And I'm sure we both can guess what he's going to say when I tell him the news."

I smiled at the thought. "Well, if you think it's for the best, then I trust your judgment."

"You do?" she asked.

"Shouldn't I?"

"You definitely should but I know you haven't been thrilled with me since the day my husband left," Kieran said.

I waved my hand. It was a topic I definitely didn't want to discuss. As far as I was concerned, Kieran likely shot or chased off her husband with the gun. One way or another, she was responsible for whatever had happened to him out there.

At the same time, I couldn't blame her after what he'd done.

"We don't need to talk about that," I said.

"Okay, then," Kieran said. "It's settled. I'll be staying with Jake and if anyone needs me, you let them know where I'll be. I'm sure Lucy blabbed it to anyone that would listen already."

"Good luck," I said.

She shook her head. "Oh, honey, I'm going to need a lot more than luck."

I chuckled as she jogged past me down the road. I watched until she safely arrived at Jake's house.

Shawn stepped out onto the porch and gestured for me to come inside. "Stevie!"

"We have to do something," I said barely turning.

"What?" he said stepping up beside me.

Either he hadn't heard me, or he was worried about what I was about to suggest. "I have to try to find his medicine."

10

———

JOSS

I stepped up beside Jenna and placed my hand on top of her arm. A long breath escaped between my lips as I pressed down, forcing her to lower the weapon.

"We're not going to kill you," I said.

"You should," the girl said. "This is just too hard. I can't take it anymore. I don't even want to do this!"

Jenna's face relaxed and she let out a sigh. The girl didn't look relieved that Jenna wasn't going to shoot her. She just sat there, blinking her round, dark eyes. Almost... disappointed.

"What's your name?" I asked.

"Allie Waters," she said. "Feel free to joke about my last name."

I ignored the suggestion. "I'm Joss and this is Jenna."

Allie nodded as she clasped her hands together in

front of herself. "I'm so incredibly sorry for taking your things. I wouldn't have done that if I would have known. Things have been so bleak. I'm starving to death." Her lips curled and she giggled. "Honestly, when I saw this place, I thought I must have died and this was my heaven. I guess that's a silly thought when everything out there has still gone to hell."

"How did you get in here?" I asked glancing toward the kitchen. I could see the front door was still locked, although she could have flipped the lock after she'd entered. My eyes popped wider. "Are you alone?"

The girl's brows curled down along with her mouth. "I'm alone. There's no one else, thank God. My experience with others hasn't been good."

She held out her arms. In the dim light, I could see she was skin and bone. There were marking some fresh and some scarred on her pale, thin arms.

"What happened?" I asked. "If you don't mind sharing."

"It's easy to get scratched up running in the darkness with no idea where you're going. The bear encounter didn't help," Allie said jerking her chin toward the gun in Jenna's lowered hand. "Just so you know, I have no idea how to use that thing. If I had, I would have tried to use it on the bear."

Jenna shrugged. "I don't really know either. At least, not really."

"I really am sorry," Allie said reaching down and picking up the jar of peanut butter. She stretched her arm toward me. "It's been a long time since I've eaten much of anything."

"We don't have much left," Jenna said.

My head bobbed. "We've been rationing what we have left."

"I feel terrible," Allie said.

I crossed my arms. "You didn't know. You couldn't have known. Still, I can't help but wonder how you got inside."

"The back door was open," Allie said.

My eyes shifted toward Jenna. She knew I was looking at her but she ignored me.

"You didn't question the candlelight?" Jenna asked.

"I didn't really think about it," Allie said. "I looked around and didn't see anyone... then I saw the food."

I left the room to check the back door. Both Jenna and Allie were silent until I returned.

"I locked it," Allie said. "I had to. It wasn't that long ago I escaped from a group of men. Terrible, awful, dreadful men."

"What happened?" I asked.

"Some things I can tell you and some I can't," Allie said. "At least not yet."

I nodded as if I understood. I did understand. There were things I wouldn't share about what I'd been through with her either. Not now. Maybe not ever.

"The men essentially have women as slaves," Allie said looking down at her mud-covered shoes. "They did all sorts of things to us. We were kept in buildings. We cooked, we cleaned, we did everything women should do. Whatever they wanted... whenever they wanted."

"There were others with you?" I asked.

"Not that escaped," Allie said. "In the houses. I left them behind. I should have helped them but I couldn't... I couldn't."

The girl was obviously traumatized by what she'd gone through. I could see it in her eyes. I didn't trust her completely but still, I could tell she was telling us the truth.

"You'll be safe here," I said.

"We'll never be safe again," Allie said.

Jenna took a step forward. "Do you think they followed you?"

"I did at first," Allie said. "But I'm not sure anymore. I've been on my own for a while."

The girl looked so sad. Her nearly black eyes filled with so much pain. Her blonde hair was coated in so much dirt that it looked almost brown.

"Why aren't you going to kill me?" Allie asked. "Who are you? What do you want from me? I'm not going to do things for you."

"We're just survivors," I said. "We're not going to make you do anything you don't want to do."

Allie shook her head. "There are no normal people left. You want something."

"How could we? You came into our house. We didn't know anyone was going to break in," I said.

"We're not going to do anything to you," Jenna said her brows squeezing together. She held up the gun between her finger and thumb. "Where did you get this?"

Allie cocked a brow. "I stole it. When I escaped. You should know I killed the guy."

I blinked. I couldn't stop looking at the petite girl, unable to imagine her harming a fly.

"I see that makes you uncomfortable," Allie said with a frown. "You should also know he deserved it. For everything he did to the women... and me."

"Would you like more peanut butter?" I asked holding out the jar.

Jenna cleared her throat before Allie could answer. "I'll see if I can find you some clean, dry clothes."

"I don't understand what's happening," Allie said. "Why are you being so nice?"

I gave her a tight-lipped smile. "Because we are nice."

"I don't know how to thank you," Allie said.

"You don't need to," I said. "We've all been in a bad place. Jenna and I didn't have help."

Allie frowned. "I can't take your food."

"We'll share what we can," I said. "Eventually, we'll have to leave here to find more."

"And if I just leave, you'll be able to stay longer," Allie said.

"We don't want that," I said. "I wouldn't be able to live with myself if you went out there and something happened."

Allie sniffed and quickly wiped away a tear. "Thank you."

She sat down on the edge of the sofa with her hands between her legs. Allie appeared to be stunned... speechless.

I came back into the room with a breakfast bar and a bottle of water. Jenna was standing at the bottom of the stairs holding a small stack of clothing.

"Should we wake her?" Jenna asked.

I shook my head. "Probably not."

"She's getting the sofa all wet," Jenna said.

"It'll dry," I said looking at the girl. Her mouth hung open slightly. It looked like it was probably the first time she'd slept in days. Maybe weeks. "Go on, get some sleep."

Jenna narrowed her eyes. "You're going to stay up?"

"Yeah," I said. "It's okay."

"Take this," Jenna said handing me the gun.

I held up my knife. She practically placed the gun in my hand.

"Just in case," Jenna said.

I shook my head. "I don't think we need to worry about her."

"Me either," Jenna said.

I sighed as I sat down next to the window. It seemed as though we had a new member of a group. Someone that needed our help. I only hoped we'd be able to help... and not make things worse.

11

ADAM

Heather started digging in her bag. She pulled out a little metal rack and a mug.

"I can help," Heather said.

"What are you going to do?" I asked as she took out a lighter.

Heather flicked it quickly and held up a packet of hot chocolate. "I don't have a lot, so you can't have one."

"Seriously? Hot chocolate?" Leah asked with a smile. "That's amazing."

Heather set it up and held the lighter under the rack. "It takes a while but I'm completely serious. This will warm you up in no time."

The lighter gave the shed a warm orange glow, highlighting the awfulness of our situation. After what felt like an eternity, Heather handed Leah the mug.

Heather packed her things away. Leah sipped the hot chocolate from the mug.

"Oh, my God," Leah said. "This is amazing. Thank you."

"Yeah, of course," Heather said.

After she finished the hot chocolate, giving us each a drink, of course, Leah fell asleep. It didn't take long before Heather curled up in the corner of the shed and found her way to dreamland too.

I couldn't sleep. I desperately needed to sleep but my eyes just wouldn't stay closed. It wasn't anything new.

There were a few brief moments I'd drifted away but the nightmares quickly woke me. I could hear Eva's voice... mocking me. Her criticisms echoing through my head.

I would never be free of her.

The gray light of morning arrived quicker than usual. At least, it seemed that way.

The yawns hit me one after the other. There were so many tears leaking out of the corners of my eyes because I was just that tired.

Leah noticed but she didn't ask what was wrong. She already knew how much I struggled with sleep.

We hadn't walked long before Leah began limping. I tried to help but she narrowed her eyes and walked quicker. She was making it clear she didn't want to talk about it and that I shouldn't mention it.

"Are you guys married?" Heather asked as we sloshed through the mud.

"No," I said quickly.

Leah raised a brow. Perhaps I had responded too quickly.

"Did you have kids?" Heather asked.

"No," Leah replied.

I chuckled. It was her turn to answer quickly.

"Are you going to have kids?" Heather asked.

"No," we both answered at nearly the exact same time.

"Okay," Heather said smiling.

I wiped the rain off the back of my neck. "Why so many questions?"

"I just want to know what to say to my uncle. He's going to want to know about the both of you," Heather said.

"Do we need to be worried about him?" I asked.

"No, no, no," Heather said shaking her head. "You'll both like him but he's built his safe place. He'll be careful about who he lets into it."

Leah and I exchanged a glance.

"Don't worry," Heather said. "It'll be fine. You'll be much safer and much happier when we get there."

"So, we're doing this?" I asked Leah when Heather was a few steps ahead of us.

"I guess so," Leah said. "It's weird, though, all this just sort of happened."

I nodded.

Heather turned abruptly and stopped. Mud splashed around her feet.

"You know, I'm just assuming he survived. I actually have no idea since we were unable to contact him after everything happened," Heather said. "Either way, I know he has the place. If he's not there, then we'll just get it all to ourselves."

Heather turned back around and started walking. She talked to us over her shoulder... the rain washed away some of her words.

"I wish I would have taken more than medicine," Heather said. "A bag full of medicine. I should have taken more. It's okay, though, because all these pills are helpful too, right? I was more interested in medicine than being a nurse. I wasn't going to have a choice but I wanted to be a pharmacist. Oh, well." Heather turned, wearing a disappointed grin. "None of that matters now, I guess. I won't get to be either. How about you, what did you want to be?"

Leah chewed her lip. "I wasn't going to have much of a choice."

"Hmm," Heather said. "What about you, Adam?"

"He would have had the luxury to choose anything he wanted," Leah said bitterly.

Heather looked impressed. "Oh, interesting! Were you going to be like a doctor or something?"

"No," I said laughing. "I didn't really know, I guess. I definitely wasn't going to be anything special."

It sounded like something Eva would have said. Or maybe she had said it. It was true, though. I wasn't going to be anything special then and I wouldn't now either.

"Adam," Leah said apologetically. "I'm sorry, I didn't mean—"

I raised my hand, stopping her from continuing. "It's fine."

And it was.

Leah never liked that I had come from an extremely wealthy family. She came from a very different world. It wasn't anything against me personally, I knew that, but still, the dislike for my past was palpable.

I probably wouldn't have liked the person I would have been either. I didn't want to think about it. The only thing I wanted to think about was finding a place that would keep us safe.

Staying alive.

My priorities had changed. Perhaps that somehow was a good thing.

The days and nights had blended together. I wasn't sure how many days had passed.

We hadn't talked much. Heather had apparently asked all her questions. Leaving us all deep in thought about our pasts... or maybe about our futures.

The food in our packs was running low. My stomach ached with my constant worry that we wouldn't find Heather's uncle's place or anywhere for that matter where we would be safe.

Everything around us was flooded and destroyed. The few remaining buildings had fallen apart. Anything inside those that still existed had been cleared out long ago.

We were in need of help.

Desperate need.

We walked past a green sign still at the side of the road. The town name had mostly worn away, making it nearly unreadable.

Heather started waving her arms and pointing. She jumped up and down, splashing the mud up so high it splattered my face.

"What are you doing?" I asked.

Heather squealed and clapped her hands. "I recognize this. I know where we are. I know the way!"

12

STEVIE

Gage wasn't thrilled but he agreed to be in charge while we were away. Shawn and I packed a bag, took a gun, and headed out to find medicine for Jake Quinn.

Tucked into the back pocket of my jeans was a small square of paper with the name of the medicine written on it. All we had to do was to carefully find a home that was still standing and search through their medicine cabinet.

Someone out there surely had used the same medicine. Whether or not it would be Jake's dosage was something we'd have to worry about later.

It seemed odd to be out traveling again... like it wasn't even me. It felt like I was back home watching myself on a TV screen.

Shawn didn't tell me how crazy I was. Instead of fighting me, he volunteered to be the one to join me.

Gage, however, didn't hold back. He let us both know that he thought we were being reckless.

I had a good night's sleep but it wasn't long before I was tired. Traveling through the mud in the cold rain was exhausting. It took a toll.

It wasn't long before we stumbled upon a two-story yellow house. The building was so soggy it looked like a stack of melting butter on top of pancakes.

"First one's the charm?" Shawn asked as we cautiously approached.

"God, I hope so," I said with a shiver.

We moved through the house quickly. Checking for both the medicine and anything else that we might need.

The house had already been picked over except for the mostly full jar of peanut butter that had fallen to the floor. I picked it up and held it like it was a first-place trophy.

"Looks like they missed something," I said.

"Nice," Shawn said raising a brow. "Should we sample it? It'll save the food we have packed."

"I think that's a great idea," I said lowering myself to the dirty floor.

I wiped my hands on my shirt and twisted off the cap. The nutty smell made my stomach rumble.

"There are no spoons," Shawn said slamming the last drawer closed.

"I don't need one," I said sticking two fingers into the jar. I closed my eyes as I let the salty, sticky, and creamy peanut butter slide onto my tongue. "Oh my God."

Shawn plopped down next to me and scooped out his own serving. "Wow. Why doesn't Kieran give us peanut butter more often?"

"I'm not about to complain about the meals she makes," I said. "But a few scoops of peanut butter would do us all good."

"Right?" Shawn said watching me as I licked my fingers clean.

My eyes narrowed. "What?"

"Nothing," Shawn said with a smirk that twisted my heart. "Watching you devour it isn't too bad either."

"Oh, my God," I groaned.

Shawn was already gone.

"Seriously," he said scooting even closer than he already was.

His thumb grazed my jaw as he moved my hair away from my face. He leaned in and placed a soft kiss on my lips.

Shawn licked and savored me as if I were his own personal spoonful of peanut butter. He eased me down to the floor and I let what was left of the jar of peanut butter roll away.

My hands slid inside his shirt and he shivered at my cool touch. Shawn's lips kissed down the side of my neck.

I exhaled as I melted into his warmth. "We should stop."

"Should we, though?" Shawn asked.

"Did you lock the door?"

"I did."

I smiled. "Still, we have a job to do."

"You're terrible at taking breaks," Shawn said as his hand slid down my body, stopping on my hip. He kissed my breast through my shirt, sending a shiver up my spine. "If you want me to stop, I'll stop. Just say the word."

A small moan seeped out between my lips. "Part of me thinks we should stop."

"What does the other part think?" he asked.

Biting my lip, I reached forward and unbuttoned his pants, giving him my answer with the gesture. Shawn smirked and reached out his hand as he got to his knees.

I took his hand and he quickly helped me to my feet. Shawn caressed my body as I wiggled out of my pants. His touch drove me crazy. I could barely think straight. All I could think about was how badly I wanted him.

Shawn placed his hands on my hips and lifted me to the counter. His hand slid up my shirt and into my bra as he shimmied out of his pants.

The tenseness in my muscles vanished. In one quick motion, he grabbed me tightly and pulled me toward him.

I gasped as I felt him take me. My fingers dug into his shoulder as the feel of him sent my pulse racing. I buried my face against his neck, closing my eyes as the world around us blurred.

I wanted to cry out his name over and over but of course, I couldn't. I had to hold every amazing feeling inside.

"Oh, Stevie," Shawn murmured into my ear. I could feel his warm breath dance along the side of my cheek. There was a desperation in his tone as he rocked into me.

We moved together as one. The cabinets banging and pounding with our movements. It was like there was an earthquake violently shaking around us.

Shawn grunted as though he were trying to hold it together a little longer. He was trying to hang onto the moment as long as possible.

But the need in his voice was enough to throw me

over the edge. I clung to him and a wave of pleasure washed around me.

My head tipped back and my lips parted. There was no stopping the sounds of pleasure that escaped. It was almost like I was possessed. I couldn't control myself.

Shawn erupted with a growl. He grabbed my hips and rolled wildly as he found his own crashing wave of bliss.

He pressed his lips to mine, kissing me until his breathing returned to normal. Shawn's eyes closed as he leaned back and let out a long breath.

Our eyes locked and he smiled. He liked losing control. A lot. "God, you're amazing."

I hopped down off the counter and pulled up my pants. I love being with him. It helped me erase everything around me but that also made me nervous. Control was something I didn't like to give up.

"Something wrong?" Shawn asked. "Not good?"

I rolled my eyes. "It was very good. We shouldn't have let our guard down like that."

"We're only human," Shawn said picking up the jar of peanut butter. He took out a big scoop with his fingers.

"I know but I have a job to do."

"We have a job to do," Shawn said handing me the

jar. "Let's not do this bickering thing again. It never ends up good."

I nodded. "Agreed."

I took another scoop before placing the lip back on the peanut butter and dropping it into my bag. Shawn sighed as he looked out the window.

I grabbed his shirt and pulled him toward me. His eyes narrowed as he looked down at my hand.

"It was awesome and I'm so glad we... took a break," I said letting my lips curl. I leaned into him and kissed his peanut-buttery lips. "Now, it's time to get back to work, though."

"Yes, ma'am," Shawn said with a smile.

I let go of his shirt. "It's too bad we weren't cele-brating having found Jake's medicine."

Shawn frowned as his head bobbed. "You're pretty worried about him, huh?"

"Very much so," I said.

"Did you hear that?" Shawn said before placing his index finger over his lips.

The only thing I'd heard had been my own voice. Shawn grabbed my hand and yanked. I dug my feet into the ground and he scowled.

I grabbed our bag and dashed to the window. Not far off, a small group of men were hooting as they shoved one another. They were coming straight toward the house.

13

JOSS

In the morning, I was startled awake. Not by the sounds of Jenna and Allie in the kitchen but by the scratching sounds outside the window.

The bear was back. I stumbled as I got to my feet.

Jenna peeked her head around the corner. "Everything okay in there, sleepyhead?"

"The bear," I managed to squeak out. "It's outside."

"Let's go then!" Jenna said excitingly. "Where's the gun?"

"You're going to shoot it?" I asked.

Jenna shrugged. "Why not?"

"What's going on?" Allie asked.

"We've been trying to catch this bear for days," Jenna said pointing to the gun. "Now's our chance."

Allie bit her lip. "I don't even know if that thing is loaded."

"Let's get under the tarp and try the ropes," I said. "If that doesn't work, you can try the gun."

"Why not gun first?" Jenna asked.

"Because if it does work, and you miss, you'll scare it off," I said.

Jenna smirked. "What makes you think I'll miss?"

"The fact that you have no idea what you're doing," I said grabbing her arm. "Come on."

Allie followed us out of the back door. The three of us carefully peeked around, making sure the bear wasn't going to lunge at us and have us for lunch. When we were sure the coast was clear, we dashed under the nearby tarp and waited.

"Make sure you remember to lock the door this time," I whispered. I turned to Allie. "No offense."

"None taken," Allie said. Her eyes scanned the yard. "I don't get it. How are you going to catch the bear?"

"We have traps set up," I said pointing at the bins that were still tilted in the same upward position we'd left them in. Then I pointed at the tree. "Rope on the ground and over the tree."

Jenna held up the thick piece of rope.

"That's never going to work," Allie said. "You can catch a bear lying on your stomach. It probably weighs a solid one-hundred-and-fifty pounds."

"Think so?" Jenna asked. "It's pretty thin."

"It's still big," Allie said.

I waved my hand at them to silence them as the bear came around the corner. It moved slowly. It grunted with each step. The darn thing seemed so unhealthy, I didn't even know if we should eat it if we did manage to catch it.

It sniffed around the back door. I held my breath when it glanced toward the tarp. Could it smell us? Hopefully, there was too much rain and water.

The bear moved around the yard, moving from side to side. It was like it knew something was different but he couldn't figure out exactly what it was.

When he stepped into the looped rope, I grabbed the end from Jenna and stood. I pulled down on the rope as hard as I could.

The rope twisted around the bear's foot but I wasn't strong enough to hoist it into the air. Jenna and Allie both stood and helped as best as they could.

"What do we do?" Jenna asked. "Should I try shooting it?"

The rain made the rope slippery but the bear wasn't able to move any closer to us than the bit of slack would allow.

"I'll do it if you want?" Allie asked.

"Okay," Jenna said handing her the gun.

Allie pointed and pulled the trigger. The sounds of clicking were followed by a sharp crack.

Allie looked at the gun as if she didn't completely understand what had happened. The cracking sound hadn't made sense but I knew instantly. The branch had snapped.

I turned just as it broke away from the tree and fell to the ground. The rope loosened and the bear charge toward us.

"Get inside!" I shouted.

We ran to the door. Jenna made it there first.

The bear, however, stepped in front of me, blocking my way. I was face to face with the angry beast and I had no idea what to do.

"Joss!" Jenna cried. After a quick look, she went inside the house, gesturing for Allie to follow.

I wasn't sure if they'd made it inside. I had to turn my attention back to the bear.

He moved to the right. I moved to the left but he was quicker and shifted his direction. He seemed to anticipate my moves.

Foamy drool dropped from its mouth to the ground as it stared at me. Hunger reddened his desperate eyes.

The bear jerked its jaw toward my left hand and snapped. I pulled my hand back only seconds before its teeth clacked together.

It was too late when I saw its claws in the air. It smacked its thick paw down against my arm.

The hot, searing pain of my skin being sliced was

like a curling iron pressed against my skin. For a moment, I couldn't see. The world around me blurred into oblivion.

"Oh my God," I said feeling dizzy as the pain traveled to my brain.

Jenna was suddenly next to me. Her hand moved impossibly quick as she screamed and slashed the bear's neck.

The bear howled before chomping in her direction. Jenna stumbled backward, landing on her bottom. The bear inched toward her, blood pouring out of its neck as it hovered over her.

"No!" I shouted punching the bear with my left fist. It didn't even seem to care. I was nothing more than an angry fly to the bear.

Allie leaped onto the bear's back. Pounding her fists on the back of its head.

"Get off her," Allie repeated over and over again.

Jenna covered her face with one arm and sliced it again with the knife. She moved it left and right and then back again. It wasn't until her fourth swing that she made contact on the side of its face near its eye.

The bear whimpered and moved back. The sudden movement threw Allie to the side.

"Oh no, you don't," Jenna said getting to her feet. She dashed toward the bear, attacking it with everything she had.

Jenna was aggressive. I turned, unable to watch. I didn't look again until I heard Jenna sobbing.

Allie had her arm around Jenna's shoulder and the bear was lifeless on the ground ten feet from them. I worked to control my breaths.

"Okay," I said between my lips. "We're okay."

Allie stared at my arm. "Your bleeding."

"Yeah," I said. "I know."

My arm shook as I held it up. There was so much blood my entire hand was coated in the deep red color.

The world around me started to get fuzzy. My head felt like it was floating. Then everything was black.

When my eyes opened, I was lying on the damp sofa with a wet washcloth on my forehead. My arm throbbed.

"She's up," Allie called.

Jenna's footsteps sounded liked thunderous booms as she came toward me. She crouched down and looked into my eyes.

"Don't like the sight of blood, huh?" I asked.

"Especially not my own," I said sitting up. I looked at the bandaging on my arm. "You did this?"

"We did," Allie said proudly.

Jenna grinned. "Found some gauze and medical tape in the upstairs bathroom. We even applied some antibiotic cream. One of the cuts looked like it needed stitches but I refrained from attempting that without your permission."

"Thanks," I said.

"You're going to be even happier when I tell you that Allie and I have started harvesting the meat from the bear," Jenna said raising her brows. "We're packing it in salt."

"How did you think of that?" I asked.

Allie pulled back her shoulders. "My kidnappers did it occasionally."

"We'll be able to stay here longer," Jenna said. "Not a lot but we bought ourselves more time."

"Maybe there will be more bears," Allie said.

Jenna nodded.

"We can't live on bear meat alone," I said.

"Are you okay?" Jenna asked. "We need to finish up with the bear meat."

"Yeah, I'm okay."

Jenna patted my knee and pointed to the bottle of water. "Drink some water. It'll help."

"Okay. Thanks."

Jenna turned and walked back toward the kitchen. She turned and looked at me over her shoulder.

"It's pretty gory in there. If you're going to pass out again, you might want to wait until we're finished," Jenna said.

"No," I said swallowed down the sour taste at the back of my throat. "I should help."

"It's okay, Joss. You were hurt pretty bad," Jenna said.

She continued toward the kitchen and stopped in the doorway. Jenna pressed her hands against the door frame and groaned.

"Are you okay?" Allie asked.

I was at her side in seconds, helping her stay upright. Her eyes met mine. They were filled with fear.

Her jaw clenched as she let out a moan from deep inside her. Jenna's eyes rolled back.

After she sucked in several quick breaths, she sighed. "It's happening again."

14

***

ADAM

Our feet moved quicker. Even Leah found a burst of energy, keeping up her pace even though she was trying to hide her limp.

About a quarter-mile ahead of us was a grouping of thick trees. All of the leaves had fallen off the gnarled, entwined branches. Mixed in with the tree trunks was the outline of a log cabin.

"We did it!" Heather squealed. "I can't believe we did it!"

She waved for us to follow as she ran ahead. I kept my eyes forward as the sourness bubbled up the back of my throat.

"Are we sure about this?" I asked.

"No, not even a little," Leah said. "But it feels like we're out of options. I can't keep going like this forever."

"We'd run out of food before coming anywhere near forever," I said.

It was like walking in a fog. I wasn't sure how we got there but we were standing on the wet ground in front of Heather's uncle's house.

She raised her fist and knocked. Heather turned to us with a big smile on her face as she bounced on the balls of her feet.

There was movement inside the house. Someone was definitely inside and I hoped to God that it was Heather's uncle. My finger's twitched and I reached my hand behind my back, ready to grab my gun.

My eyes darted around. It felt like we were eyes on us... studying us.

I sucked in a breath when the door flung open. My fingers wrapped around the handle of the gun.

"Uncle Eli!" Heather squeaked.

He grabbed her and lifted her off her feet before wrapping his arms around her thin body. "Heather? Is that you?"

"It's me all right!" Heather said as he lowered her down to the ground. "These are my friends Leah and Adam."

"Well, come on in out of the rain already," Uncle Eli said. He pointed at a mat on the floor next to the door. "Take off your shoes."

We all removed our mud-covered shoes carefully. After, he shook Leah's hand and then mine.

"Eli," he said tightly gripping my hand.

"Adam," I responded with a respectful nod. "Nice to meet you. Nice place you have here."

I'd barely taken a look. The way I'd been raised was making a brief appearance. Be polite. Mind your manners.

"Thanks," Eli said. "It's not much but I like it."

"I love it," Heather said.

The cabin was in pristine condition. Everything was clean and neatly arranged. The three of us stood there, making a mess on Eli's floor.

"Let me get you some towels so you can dry off," Eli said placing his hand on Heather's shoulder. He leaned closer but I could still hear his booming, deep voice. "Where's your ma and pa?"

Heather frowned. "They didn't make it."

"Oh," Eli said.

"I wish I didn't have to be the one to tell you that," Heather said.

Eli patted her gently. "Lots of people didn't make it. I assumed the worst for you and your parents so you can imagine my surprise seeing you again. I'm very happy you're here."

"I can't believe we found our way here," Heather said.

"Where are you all from?" Eli asked over his shoulder as he pulled out a stack of towels.

"California," I said.

Eli turned, his mouth dropping. "No kidding?"

"I kind of wish I was," I said with a chuckle.

"That's quite a journey. What made you come this way?" Eli asked.

"It's all gone," I said. "Earthquakes... flooding."

Eli's head bobbed. "It was one massive shit-storm, huh?"

"Indeed," I said.

"Well, you'll be safe here," Eli said. "It gets cold at night. I don't like using the fireplace because of the smoke it makes but I have lots of blankets. Haven't had a single visitor out this way until now and I'd like to keep it that way."

"I don't blame you," I said looking around.

There was a sofa and a few chairs made out of wood that matched the stain on the interior wooden walls. A rather large fireplace sat in the middle of the living room. There were a few pictures on the mantle and the head of a deer mounted above it.

"Not a fan of people," Eli admitted. "Especially these days. Can't trust anyone."

"Couldn't agree more," I said crossing my arms. "That's something I learned rather quickly."

"If you want us to leave...," Leah said taking a step toward the door.

Eli flapped his hand, waving away her words. "Nonsense. Friends of Heather's are friends of mine. I meant I don't like strange people. The ones that poked around early on. They just wanted to take, take, take."

"I thought you said you haven't had any visitors?" Leah asked.

Eli's head turned sharply. "I should have been clearer. None that have been allowed to stick around. Heather isn't a stranger. She's my niece."

"Oh," Leah said.

"It's not a mistake I'll make again. Luckily, it was only a handful of people. I'm pretty well hidden out here," Eli said handing us each two towels. "I've got a couple rooms to spare. I'll show you where you can put your things after you've dried off."

"We appreciate that," I said before drying my hair as best as I could with the towel.

Eli stood there watching us, eyeing each drop of water that fell from our clothing. He cringed when his eyes settled on the mess at our feet.

"Do you have dry clothing?" Eli asked.

"Yeah," Leah said.

She had packed some before we'd left the resort but we didn't have much. Leah had wanted to save the room for things that were more important, like food and clean water.

"Excellent," Eli said holding out his hand. "This way."

The three of us followed him single file. He stopped at the first door. "This is the bathroom." To the right were two more doors. "Bedroom one and bedroom two. Take your pick."

Heather lunged forward. "I'll take the one by the bathroom."

"That leaves you two with this one," Eli said. "Hope sharing is okay? Otherwise, I have the—"

"Sharing is fine," Leah replied hastily.

"Perfect. Meals are served at eight, noon, and five," Eli pointed to a large clock hanging on the wall near the dining room table.

The layout of the cabin was a big open space except for the rooms. There were a few more doors, which I assume were Eli's bedroom and closets.

"I carefully ration the food," Eli said. "It could be years before things get anywhere back to normal. I'm sure you understand."

"Yes, of course," I said pushing my shoulders back.

I was tempted to donate what we had in our bags but I wasn't sure how long we'd be allowed to stay. There was a chance we would need what was in them.

"Thank you so much for everything, Uncle Eli," Heather said clasping her hands together.

"You bet, kid," Eli said. "You're all welcome to stay as long as you like but I should warn you. It's not fun. There isn't anything to do but sit around and wait for time to pass."

What Eli may not have realized was that it was like that everywhere. Just some places were more dangerous than others.

"Well," Eli said rubbing his rough palms together. "I have some work to attend to."

"Right. Of course," I said reaching out my hand to shake again. "Thanks so much for your hospitality. We really appreciate it."

Eli grunted and snatched the towels from us. I watched him as I started to close the door. He was down on his hands and knees, wiping up the mess before I had the door halfway closed.

I locked the door and yawned. Leah was pulling out clothing for us.

The room was like a small hotel room but it was plenty of space for the two of us. There was a wooden dresser with a mirror, a large walk-in closet, and a king-sized bed. Near the only window in the room was a desk and a chair.

"We should change," Leah said setting down my

outfit on the bed. "He seemed really nervous, didn't he?"

"I don't think he liked the mess we made," I said.

"I don't think he likes us at all," Leah said.

I shrugged. "He's apprehensive. Can you blame him?"

"No," Leah said. "But it's making me jittery... like I just drank an entire pot of coffee."

"Maybe he's just a nervous guy," I said. "I mean, he did have this place before everything happened. Clearly, he liked being hidden away."

"I don't know if we should stay here," Leah said.

My finger moved along my chin. "You need to heal. We'll give it some time."

Leah peeled off her shirt and quickly pulled on the dry one. She folded up the wet clothes and looked around for somewhere to set them where they wouldn't touch anything that belonged to Eli. After a moment, she placed them on top of our bags in the corner of the room.

Her eyes moved around as if she were looking for something. My brow wrinkled as I watched her.

"What are you doing?" I asked.

"I know it's totally crazy but it feels like I'm being watched," Leah said.

I understood the feeling. "It's just because we're in

this new place. And our past experiences probably aren't helping matters."

"You're probably right," Leah said sitting down on the edge of the bed. She folded her hands in her lap. "I don't feel like I should touch anything. It's all so... perfect."

The hard knock at the door startled me. I took a quick step back and tried to ignore the pounding in my chest.

Leah stood, gesturing at me to get the door. I pushed back my shoulders and inhaled deeply before opening the door.

The smile on my face pinched the muscles in front of my ears. It felt like I was a puppet whose strings were being jerked too hard.

"Hey there, Eli," I said in an awkward, slightly higher pitch. I cleared my throat, still smiling.

Eli stared at me and blinked once. "Come with me. I want to show you something."

15

STEVIE

We ran out the back door and hid in a thick shrub. The little twigs scratched and stabbed at me through my clothing. I winced as one of the little branches sliced my cheek.

Blood smeared on the back of my hand as I wiped at the stinging cut. Shawn looked at me, his eyes focused on my cheek.

"I'm fine," I whispered.

Shawn nodded. Surely, he could see it was just a scratch. "Think they can see us?"

"I sure as hell hope not," I said scooting myself deeper into the torturous bush.

I couldn't hear or see the men but I knew they were in the house. The rain picked up and fell harder, creating a mist around us. It was the first time I was thankful for the strange weather.

It was crazy to think about all the devastation caused by a device they hoped would help with climate change. Everything destroyed by one single choice.

One single event that we likely wouldn't ever know more about. Most everyone was gone. The only thing that mattered now was survival.

Would the rain ever stop? I hoped so.

Would we ever see the sun again? I hoped so, because if we didn't, life wouldn't continue.

I couldn't think about it. It wasn't like there was anything any of us could do about it anyway. I exhaled as I wiped away the droplets of rain off my face.

"What if they stay there?" I asked.

"Then I guess we live in this bush now," Shawn said.

He snapped his mouth shut when the men walked out the back door. They were laughing and having a good ol' time.

There were four men and one bottle of what I assumed was vodka. Their jovial mood could likely be attributed to the liquor, which could quite possibly mean it would be a disaster if they found us.

They started walking toward us. I froze, hoping the mist was hiding us.

"Wait!" one of the men said bursting out, laughing as he slapped one of the others on the back. "This is the wrong way."

"Are you sure?" the second guy asked.

"I'm like sixty percent sure."

They all laughed. "Then we better turn around."

The men turned and walked away.

I didn't take in a full breath until they were gone. "That was close."

"Yeah, but truth be told, I wasn't that worried," Shawn said raising the gun slightly. "I'm pretty sure I could have taken them all."

"Yeah, maybe," I said. "But maybe not before someone accidentally got killed."

I carefully backed out of the shrub and stared up at the sky. We couldn't go back. Not yet. And not without Jake's medicine.

It seemed to me that there was one way that would ensure that we'd find it but it wouldn't be easy. It also wouldn't be safe.

"I have an idea," I said even though I wasn't entirely sure how I was going to tell Shawn what I was thinking. Maybe there was a part of me that was only telling him because I knew he'd talk me out of it.

"What's your idea?" Shawn said crossing his arms. He looked up at the sky as if he'd see the answer.

"Before you say no, hear me out."

Shawn's brow wrinkled. "Okay."

"We need to get medicine for Jake, right?"

"Right."

"There is a place we can check for the medicine and it's more likely to have it. Quicker and easier than roaming around checking random looted houses," I said.

Shawn threaded his arms together in front of his chest. I could tell he already didn't like what I was going to say.

"We can do it smart and careful," I said.

"Just forget it," Shawn said.

"I think I have to try," I said. "I know it's stupid and dangerous but there is a good chance it's our only option."

Shawn shook his head. "It's not happening. We're not doing it."

"Well, I'm doing it," I said as I turned and walked away from him.

"No, you're not," Shawn said jogging to catch up with me. "Gage would kill me if I allowed it."

I snorted. "It's not like you're in charge here. You're not *allowing* me to do anything. I'm just doing it."

"Stevie, think this through," Shawn said.

"I did," I said stubbornly.

"Give it more than twenty seconds of thought," Shawn pleaded.

Perhaps he was right. I hadn't really given it a lot of thought but I also didn't see any other way. It wasn't like I could go back home without the medicine.

"How about this, we go close enough to see if finding medicine is even an option? If they left the medicine at the pharmacy, maybe it's possible to get in and get out without even being seen," I said.

"We don't know our way around," Shawn said. He shook his head. "This is like the worst idea ever."

"Feel free to go back," I said barely flicking him a glance.

Shawn chuckled. "Not a chance."

"Then let's do this," I said.

"You're absolutely sure?" Shawn asked.

I checked my pocket to make sure I still had the piece of paper with the medicine's name on it. "I'm sure."

"Jake wouldn't want us to do this," Shawn said.

"I have to do this for him. We have to do everything we can for our people," I said. "We work together. We're going to watch each other's back. That's what we do. I'm convinced that's why Gage and I made it this far. All of us."

"Okay. Let's do it then," Shawn said. "I trust you."

I nodded as I let out a breath. I was surprised he hadn't put up more of a fight.

"Okay," I said taking a step.

Shawn stuck out his arm to stop me. I turned to look at him.

"We're just checking it out. If for any reason we're in danger, we leave, right?" Shawn said.

"Sure," I replied. I smiled at him. "I'm not going to let anything happen to you."

Shawn huffed. "Sometimes, you're impossible."

I shrugged. I was who I was. If someone was in need of help, I wasn't able to walk away—especially someone like Jake Quinn.

Without further discussion, we headed north.

16

JOSS

Allie and I helped Jenna to the sofa. The contractions happened three more times before they seemed to stop.

"I can't believe this is happening again," Jenna said looking into my eyes. "I think they stopped for now, though."

"Good," I said. "But maybe this isn't the same as before."

Jenna's eyebrows formed a thick line. "Are you trying to scare me?"

"No, I just mean... well, the baby could actually come soon, right?" I asked.

"Oh," Jenna said. "Um, I don't know. I lost all track of time. It stopped, though, so I guess it's not time."

I smiled at her. "It's probably whatever it was that doctor told you."

"I wish it wasn't so painful," Jenna said.

"I've never had kids but I've heard it's painful," I replied.

Jenna exhaled. "I never really thought about what it would be like. Most of the time, I tried to ignore the fact that I was pregnant."

"We'll figure it out," I said.

I helped Allie in the kitchen while Jenna rested. It turned out that the bear's blood didn't bother me. Apparently, it was only my own that caused me to get lightheaded.

"I'll get some more water from out back," I said. "It'll probably take several trips before this mess is cleaned up."

"Sorry," Allie said.

"It's fine. The meat will help us," I said.

I carefully looked out the window before stepping outside. A shiver ran down my spine when the rain hit me.

I walked over to the side of the house where we collected the rain that dripped off the roof. Instead of picking up the pail, I leaned back against the siding and covered my face.

Tears streamed down my cheeks. I was worried sick about Jenna. The world we were living in was just too hard. I couldn't take care of her.

I had no idea when winter would come but I knew

that we wouldn't survive when it did. We weren't prepared for anything beyond a few weeks.

It was stupid of us to think we would have a chance to survive. All we'd been doing was delaying the inevitable. And now, with Allie here, we had another mouth to feed.

What the hell were we thinking?

It wasn't like we could have turned her away. She's been nothing but helpful, although a bit shy but really, who could blame her? We didn't know much about her but it sounded like she'd been to hell and back.

My arms fell to my side and I looked up at the sky. I let the rain wash down over my face.

"What should I do?" I asked as more tears fell. Robby would have known what to do.

I desperately wanted him to answer my question… to guide me, but of course, I knew he couldn't.

I missed him so much.

"Why did you have to go?" I asked as if Robby would suddenly appear.

Squishy footsteps caused my spine to straighten so quickly it popped between my shoulder blades. Allie cautiously peeked around the corner.

"Everything okay?" she asked.

I quickly wiped the rain and tears from my face. "Yeah, sorry."

"I started to get worried," Allie said.

"Sorry. I guess I got distracted."

"Who were you talking to?" Allie asked looking around.

I pulled in a shaky breath. I didn't know what to say or where to start but somehow, the words started flowing.

She nodded as I told her everything from the store to seconds before he died. I didn't tell her about the ring. For some reason, I wanted to keep that to myself.

"I'm so sorry," Allie said. "I hope you don't take this the wrong way but it's better to have loved than to never have loved at all. I've never had anything like that in my life."

"It's so hard to keep going without him here," I said. "And without Caleb too."

"They sound like they were really special people. I wish I could have known them," Allie said.

I looked away from her, so I didn't start bawling. "It's so hard to lose someone you love that much. I feel like I'm missing a part of myself. Anyway, I just want a few minutes. I'll be in soon, okay?"

"Sure," Allie said quickly placing her hand on my shoulder. "If you do ever want to talk, though, I'm here to listen."

"Thanks," I said. I had no desire to talk to anyone. It was a mistake. I'd blurted out everything. Life was easier if I didn't allow myself to think about him.

"I get it, though," Allie said. "I haven't talked to anyone about what happened to me when I was captured. It's like I forgot how to be normal."

I slowly breathed as the memories of everything started to fade. Everything around me began to clear and I remember where I was... in the painful present.

"Anyway, sorry for upsetting you," Allie said as she walked away.

I huffed. "It wasn't your fault. I was already upset."

My voice had been soft. She probably hadn't even heard me. I had no idea why I had just spilled everything to a complete stranger.

I was tired. That was probably why.

After Allie left, I took in several deep breaths. I refused to let my mind wander back to him. I couldn't fall apart. Not now.

We finished cleaning the kitchen while Jenna rested. I made a small meal for Allie and me and a bigger one for Jenna. If she noticed the portion size difference, she didn't mention it.

Allie thanked me repeatedly. "So, delicious. Let me clean the dishes."

"Really?"

"Yeah," Allie said. "Of course."

I worried because I didn't want her to feel like Jenna or I were forcing her to help. The last thing I wanted was for her to feel like she was here to serve us.

"If you don't mind. It would be a big help and I'm totally exhausted," I said.

"Yeah, it's fine. Go get some sleep," Allie said with a wave of her hand. "Sleep away those dark circles under your eyes."

I laughed. "Pretty sure at this point, they are permanent."

"Try anyway," Allie said with a smile.

"If you insist," I said.

"Help me up," Jenna said.

I easily got her to her feet as Allie left the room. "Should we really leave her unsupervised?"

"Don't be a worrywart," Jenna said. She lowered her voice. "We'll lock our door, just in case."

"Ah, we just give the illusion of trust," I said.

Jenna covered her laugh before it could escape. "I actually like having her here."

"I do too," I said. "It's less lonely."

"She's a distraction," Jenna said with a frown.

"Are you feeling any better?" I asked letting the seriousness soak into my face.

Jenna's lips curled up. "Much. I guess maybe I've just been doing too much."

"Probably," I said holding her waist as we climbed the stairs side by side. "Sleep will do us both good."

I locked the bedroom door. Jenna flopped into bed while I searched for a set of dry clothes to sleep in.

She was sleeping before I even undressed. It seemed as though the pain she experienced had worn her out.

It was early morning when I was awoken by a scream. My hand patted the empty space on the bed next to me.

"Jenna?" I said popping out of bed.

I bolted down the stairs. Jenna was on the sofa, her legs wide as she held her stomach and howled.

Allie paced frantically, hesitating when she saw me. "I think she's in labor."

17

ADAM

I followed Eli to a door at the back of the kitchen. He pulled open the door and gestured at the stairs.

"You want me to go down?" I asked.

"Uh, yeah," Eli said.

"Okay," I said sucking in a breath as I turned my back to Eli.

Eli was a big guy. He was tall and cleanly shaved. Eli was half college professor and half lumberjack and fully intimidating.

There was a hum that grew louder as I descended the stairs. It wasn't dark... there was a slight glow. I turned the corner and entered Eli's spectacular bunker.

"Holy crap," I said. The lights flickered and grew brighter, illuminating the entire room. "Lights?"

"Generator," Eli said his lips curling at the ends.

"Why don't you stay down here?" I asked.

Eli shifted his weight. "This is just for an emergency."

I was tempted to ask what he considered what had happened to be. If the world we were living in wasn't an emergency situation, I didn't know what was. But I kept my mouth shut.

"Don't tell my niece but I think things will get worse," Eli said. "Humanity will destroy itself but I'm not going to go down with it."

"So, what's your plan?" I asked.

"We'll wait it out," Eli said as if the answer was obvious. "Eventually, years from now, perhaps it will be safe again. You know what it's like out there, tell me I'm wrong."

I couldn't. "Have you been out at all?"

"No," Eli said laughing. "I'm not an idiot. No offense."

"None taken," I said as my eyes scanned the underground house. "If I would have had a choice, I wouldn't have gone out either."

"I didn't bring you down here to talk about what's going on out there," Eli said.

I cocked my head. "Why did you bring me down here?"

"I wanted to talk to you about the weapons the two of you are carrying," Eli said. "I don't particularly feel safe for my niece or myself with the two of you carrying."

"I don't know how safe I feel without it," I said raising a brow. "No offense. I appreciate you letting us stay here but I don't know you. Other than what Heather has told us."

Eli smirked. "What has she told you?"

"Not a lot," I admitted.

"Follow me," Eli said. He opened a closet and took out a metal case. "I wonder if you'd be willing to keep your guns here. It's not locked and you'll know exactly where they are. You aren't going to need them while you're at my house."

"If it's all the same, I'd like to keep my girlfriend and me safe," I said.

Eli exhaled, scratching the back of his neck. "It's not all the same. Here's the thing, if anyone comes close to the cabin, I'll know about it. There are booby-traps and cameras at various locations. I keep that powered twenty-four-seven."

"You saw us coming." My thought leaked out.

"I did," Eli said.

"How the hell did we avoid your traps?" I asked.

Eli rolled his shoulders. "I deactivated them... for my niece. Look, Adam, let me take the guns. If you want to leave, you can take them back. I don't need your guns, I have plenty of my own."

I drew in a breath that vibrated my chest. Did I

even have a choice in the matter? If we stayed, which we needed to do because of Leah's injury, I had to give them up. If I didn't give them up, we'd have to leave and Leah definitely wasn't in any condition for that.

"Fine," I said. "And you'll leave them right here?"

"I will," Eli said holding up the case.

I placed my gun inside even though I knew it was going to upset Leah. I ran my hand down my face and groaned.

"I need your girlfriend's gun too," Eli said. "Why don't you go on and get it while I wait."

I turned and went up the stairs, already regretting that I'd made the decision without talking to Leah first. She wasn't going to be happy.

"Are you nuts?" she asked when I asked for her gun.

I closed the door and tapped my index finger on my lips. "You need to heal. We won't make it far with your injured leg. I don't like it any more than you do but we need a break."

"What if he won't give them back?" Leah asked.

"Maybe we won't need them back," I said pressing my hands against my face. "I'm sorry, I screwed up. I didn't know what else to do. What should I have done?"

Leah's shoulders fell. Her eyes darted around, eventually settling on a spot on the floor.

"I don't know," Leah said. She came over to me and wrapped her arms around my neck. "I'm sorry. I don't know why I'm being so hard on you."

"It's okay," I said. "This isn't easy."

"You've been nothing but perfect to me," she said. "I'm the jerk. Can you forgive me?"

I looked lazily into her eyes. "Already done. I know you're just looking out for us."

"I should tell you, though," I said pulling back slightly. I lowered my voice. "Eli has a massive gun collection down there."

"I'm worried that this was a mistake," Leah said.

"We'll figure something out," I said placing a kiss on her forehead.

Leah sighed and rested her head on my shoulder. "Those guns were all we had keeping us safe."

"We can collect them and leave when you're healed," I said swallowing down a yawn. "And after I've gotten some sleep. I'm not at the top of my game."

"I know," Leah said twisting her fingers into my hair.

"I really don't think he'll keep our guns," I said. "He has no use for them. He could supply a small army with what he has down there."

Leah's head bobbed. "What's it like down there?"

"It's truly unbelievable." I smiled. "It's like, down

there, nothing changed. Of course, you can't ever leave or you'd know the truth."

"There is one good thing that came out of all of this," Leah said.

"There is?"

She pressed her warm lips to mine. I should have thrown her down on the bed but I forced myself to gently pull away.

"Mmm," I said brushing my thumb along Leah's lower lip. "I don't want to leave but if I don't bring your gun down to him, he'll probably come knocking."

Leah pressed her lips together and turned away. "We don't want that, do we?"

"I'll be right back," I said.

"I'm not going anywhere," she said pulling up her pant leg. She frowned at her injury. "I should probably have Heather take another look. It looks worse."

"Yeah, maybe you should," I said. "Wish I could help but I don't have the supplies. I'll see what Eli has when I bring him your gun."

I left the room, heading back down to the bunker. Eli was standing in the same spot, impatience wrinkled his brow.

"That took a while," Eli said. "I want to make sure I start dinner on time."

"Sorry," I said. "Do you have anything for treating a wound?"

"What kind of wound?" Eli asked.

"A deep cut," I said. "Leah slipped and cut herself on a piece of metal."

Eli stroked his chin. "Is it infected?"

"I hope not," I said.

"I'll take a look," Eli said. "Then, dinner."

"Thanks," I said. "Is there anything I can do to help?"

Eli narrowed his eyes.

"With dinner."

"My supplies are my business," Eli said. "You eat what I make. That's the deal."

"Sorry," I said holding up my hands. "I didn't mean for it to sound like I was snooping. I only wanted to help."

He shook his head as he pointed to the stairs. "I don't need help. Go."

18

STEVIE

We hid in a house for the night. I didn't know how close to the town we were but we needed to rest before even attempting to go near it. We'd need to be ready for anything, especially when only one of us was armed.

As we cautiously approached the town, keeping ourselves as hidden as possible, doubt started to bubble in my stomach. How big of a mistake was I making?

The buildings at the edge of town seemed empty. There weren't a lot of hiding places but we stayed close to the house as we moved deeper into the town.

It wasn't a place I was familiar with but it was likely the pharmacy would be closer to downtown. We hid behind a tree trunk when we heard voices.

Three men walked by without noticing us. They

entered a building at nearly the same moment another man exited a building down the road.

"Half of them are armed," Shawn said.

"I noticed." I gestured around the area. "It seems as though they're all staying around here."

We weren't far from the edge of town. For whatever reason, the men occupied a grouping of houses in what used to be a gated community.

"Maybe we can get to the pharmacy without being seen," I said.

"But which way?" Shawn asked.

"Not sure," I said studying our surroundings.

I watched the men move from building to building. I had no idea what they were doing but I tried to count them. It was hard but an estimation of how many people lived in the area seemed like something that would be good to know.

Of course, there could be people in the buildings that weren't coming out. The best I could do was estimate.

"How many people you think are living there?" I asked.

"More than twenty," Shawn said.

I nodded. "Less than fifty?"

"Yeah," Shawn said. "I agree with that."

"Maybe this will be easier than I thought," I said jerking my chin to the left.

We headed closer to town and away from the community. Shawn kept the gun ready.

Shawn and I carefully weaved our way through the streets. The town, however, was too big. We had no idea which way to go.

"Maybe we should leave and come back after we talk to Jake," Shawn suggested. "We're just running around like chickens with our heads cut off. Every minute we stay puts us more at risk."

"Gage will never let us come back," I said pointing at another street.

I shook my head with frustration. The town wasn't nearly as big as I had thought. Before we knew it, we were on the opposite side of where the men were staying.

"Let's go back," I said.

Shawn grabbed my arm. "Stevie, no."

"What do you mean, no? We're so close," I said.

"We'll get the information we need and come back," Shawn said. "And we can be more prepared when we do."

I closed my eyes and let out a heavy breath. "One more look, okay?"

"Let's just get out while we can and come up with a plan," Shawn said.

"But we're right here," I said throwing my hands in the air. "How can we just leave?"

"We'll figure out a way, okay?" Shawn said pleading with his slanted eyebrows. "I promise we'll come back and we'll get Jake's medicine."

I shook my head. "This is ridiculous. He needs it now, not days from now."

"Shh!" Shawn said aggressively tapping his finger to his lips. "I trusted you and came here. Now it's time you trust me. It's time to leave."

On some level, I knew he was right but I didn't like it. I desperately wanted to have the medicine when we returned.

"Fine," I said unable to stop my shoulders from dropping. I felt as though I'd been in a boxing match and had lost.

We left the town, heading south around the outskirts. I stopped and turned back, looking at the town as if maybe there would be a flashing neon light in the sky, directing me to the pharmacy.

I sighed and turned back, noticing that Shawn hadn't realized I'd stopped walking. I took several quick steps to catch back up to him but suddenly, the world whooshed past my face.

Everything spun and twisted. My stomach felt like it went from my feet to my throat and then back again. I wasn't sure what had happened as my body bobbed up and down before settling to a gentle swinging motion.

It was as though I'd fallen through the earth. Everything was upside down. My eyes frantically darted around and my head tingled as I searched to find Shawn in the falling rain.

"Shawn," I whispered as I noticed the faint sounds of a bell.

I tried to reach up but I didn't have the strength to grab the rope twisted around my ankle. My eyes finally locked with Shawn's below.

"Get me down," I said.

Our bag was hanging off my back awkwardly. I couldn't remember if we'd taken anything sharp that he could use to cut me down.

"Throw down the bag," Shawn said.

I could tell by the look on his face that he didn't know what we had either. What I did know was that he didn't have anything other than the gun. Shooting me down wasn't an option.

The sounds of the bell didn't get louder but each ring pierced my ears. I hurried as I shrugged my shoulders to get the bag to slide off my arms.

It plopped down in the mud only seconds before I heard voices. Shawn's eyes widened. He had heard them too.

"You have to go," I said.

"No," Shawn said stubbornly. "I'm not leaving you."

The tingling in my brain grew stronger. "Please, Shawn. Go. If you don't, you won't be able to help me. You can't get caught."

"I can't," Shawn said between heavy, fear-filled breaths.

"Please," I begged. "Go."

Shawn ran his hands through his hair. He raised the gun as if he was going to fight. He must have seen something that changed his mind.

Shawn picked up the bag and flung it over his shoulder. "I'll be back, okay? I'll be back for you. I promise."

"Okay," I said. "Run. Before they see you."

Shawn took a step and stopped. He looked at me over his shoulder. "I love you."

I bit my cheek to stop myself from crying. Watching him run away from me was incredibly painful. It was one of the hardest things I'd ever had to endure.

My eyes closed as I tried to telepathically send him a message. "I love you too."

19

———————

JOSS

My brow wrinkled as I knelt down on the floor next to Jenna's leg. "Why didn't you wake me up?"

"I'm not in labor," Jenna said her voice a bit lower than usual. "It's just the pains again."

"Are you sure?" I asked. "This seems different."

"No, no," Jenna said.

Her breaths started to come quicker. She leaned forward and shouted as she held her stomach.

I glanced at Allie over my shoulder. It was apparent by her tightly pressed together lips and wide eyes she was thinking the same thing I was... the baby was coming.

"Can you help me?" I asked looking into Allie's eyes.

"There's nothing to help with," Jenna said.

Allie nodded.

"Stop it, you two," Jenna said sucking in quick breaths. "It's too early. At least I think it's too early."

"Wouldn't you rather we were ready just in case?" I asked.

"You have no idea how to deliver a baby," Jenna said reminding me of something I was fully aware of.

I crossed my arms. "Fine. Good luck."

"No, wait!" Jenna said leaning forward. "Fine, prepare yourself but I'm telling you this is going to pass."

"What do we do?" Allie asked.

"Oh, God. I'm going to die, aren't I?" Jenna asked staring up at the ceiling. Her hands clenched into fists as she started cursing. "What the hell are you waiting for!"

Allie's brow squished together. "Pain medicine?"

"I don't know if she can have it." I frowned as I twisted my fingers. "Okay, um, let's get towels and blankets. Clean ones only."

"Water?" Allie asked.

I nodded. "The boiled water."

"What else?" Allie asked.

"I'm not sure," I said shaking my head. "Let's just get that collected first."

"And hurry!" Jenna shouted as we left the room.

I bolted up the stairs to the linen closet. I was terrified something was going to go wrong but somehow, I was managing to keep it together.

If I freaked out... Jenna would freak out. We couldn't have that. We all just needed to stay calm.

I put the pillows on the floor, along with the sofa cushions and several musty smelling blankets that probably hadn't been used in years. Hopefully, they would be clean enough for Jenna to lie on.

Allie and I helped her to the floor only seconds before the next contraction. They were coming fast. There was absolutely no doubt in my mind that the baby was coming.

"I can't do this," Jenna said grabbing my hand. "I'm not going to make it. I'm not strong enough."

I smiled and shook my head. "Yes, you can. You're going to do great."

"I don't know what made me think I could do this," Jenna said. "I thought I'd have more time."

Her eyes squeezed together and her teeth clenched as another contraction found her. Allie and I held her hands as she leaned forward, her legs wide as if they already knew what they'd have to do.

"Okay," I said after she relaxed and leaned back into the pillows. "You're going to have to take your pants off."

"Buy me dinner first," Jenna growled.

"I don't want to do this anymore than you do," I said.

Allie helped her out of her clothing and covered her with a sheet. I kneeled between her legs.

"It's coming. It's coming. It's coming," Jenna repeated over and over again.

"Okay," I said pressing my hands together. "I'm going to have a look."

"Do it then!" Jenna shouted. "I don't know what the hell you're waiting for. A written invitation?"

I blinked several times. "I'm not the one that got you pregnant. Don't take it out on me."

"Sorry," Jenna said starting to cry. Seconds later, she was mad that she was crying. "Just help me already!"

"Holy crap," I said quickly covering my mouth.

"What's wrong?" Jenna asked her words running together.

I shook my head. "Nothing. I see the baby. It really is coming."

"I need to push," Jenna said.

"Okay," I said pulling in a slow breath to ready myself. "Push."

Of course, I had no idea if she should push or not. All I could do was assume that whatever felt natural for her was hopefully the right thing to do.

Jenna pushed again. She screamed and cried and shouted. And just like that, the baby's head was out.

"The head is out!" I said excitedly.

I tried to hold on to the slippery baby while also being extremely careful. I'd never held a baby, at least not one as young as Jenna's was.

"Give me a towel," I said.

Allie handed me a bright yellow towel. The color seemed unusual because of how much it stood out in our environment. Everything was gray and dreary but the towel seemed overly colorful.

The baby slipped out with the next push. He was anxious to get out and into this world. Too bad I couldn't have warned him. Maybe he would have wanted to wait a bit longer.

He was so tiny. His little hands were wiggling but he didn't cry.

"It's a boy!" I said.

Jenna sat up, trying to see him. "Is he okay?"

"He's moving," I said.

"Why isn't he crying?" Jenna asked.

"I'm not sure," I said. "Ready to hold him?"

Jenna bit her lip. "Um, I don't know."

"You are," I said confidently.

Jenna took him into her arms, wrapping the towel tightly around him. She held him against her chest and he started to cry.

"Guess he likes you better," Jenna said lightly brushing the wet hair at her temple away from her eye.

"Nonsense," I said.

"What do I do now?" Jenna asked.

I shrugged.

"Umbilical cord," Allie said. "We have to cut that. Oh, and the placenta."

Jenna and I both looked at Allie. Allie flashed us a nervous smile.

"I've helped a couple other women," Allie said. "When I was with the other group. I didn't do much but I was there. We'll need something to clamp it."

"What do I do about the placenta?" Jenna asked.

"We just wait," Allie said.

Jenna looked down at the baby. She smiled at him.

"Isn't he the most beautiful baby you've ever seen?" Jenna asked.

"Definitely," I replied.

Allie got up and dashed to the kitchen. I could hear her going through the drawers and cabinets.

"I can't believe he's real," I said lightly touching his forehead.

"We're going to take really good care of you," Jenna said. "Me and your aunt Joss."

I shook my head. "That's not necessary."

"You'll get used to aunt Joss." Jenna leaned closer and whispered something to him.

"What did you say?" I asked.

"Nothing important," Jenna said widening her smile. "I have a name for him."

I blinked. "Already?"

"I've thought about it for a while now."

"Oh yeah?"

"Yeah." Jenna nodded. "I'm going to call him Cal but his name is Caleb Robert."

The lump in my throat made my eyes burn. It was the perfect name. It was just too bad Caleb and Robby weren't around to hear the name.

"Think they'd like it?" Jenna asked.

"I think they'd love it."

After everything was finished and Allie and I had cleaned up, we all sat in the living room. Jenna had attempted to feed her baby but it didn't seem as though there was anything for him to drink. It didn't matter because he seemed content.

I held Cal when Jenna could barely keep her eyes open. It was hard to understand how something so small could bring a smile to my face when outside was nothing but awfulness and dread.

"I don't want to stop looking at him," she said.

"I don't blame you," I said.

It wasn't long before exhaustion overtook both her and Allie. Somehow, I felt more awake than I had in a long time. Perhaps it was the adrenaline that still seemed to be coursing through my body.

"Caleb Robert," I whispered when I was sure the other two were sleeping. "You sure chose an interesting time to come into this world."

I stared at him. He brought his hand to his mouth and gently gnawed on his closed fist.

"You're hungry, huh? Yeah, unfortunately, that's the way of this world. Your mom will be able to keep you fed, though. Let's just let her sleep a little longer, okay?" I whispered.

Cal wouldn't know a world any different from the one we were in. He'd grow up used to the rain. He wouldn't even know what the sun was or how it felt on a summer day.

The baby would never know about the cars or the internet. Maybe it was better that he didn't. It would be easier to live when you didn't know everything you were missing.

"I'm going to do everything I can to keep you and your mom safe," I whispered. The words had just seeped out of my mouth. I hadn't given them any thought. "I will protect you until the day I die."

It was true, though. I would do anything to keep little Cal safe. I didn't know him but for some reason, I felt a strong bond with the little guy.

Jenna cleared her throat.

I sucked in a breath and my eyes connected with hers. "I thought you were asleep."

"I was," she said. "But your noisy conversation woke me up."

"Sorry," I whispered.

"Actually, my boobs kind of hurt," Jenna said. "I think I should try to feed him again."

I carefully stood and held Cal until she was situated. "Ready?"

"Yep," Jenna said. She held him to her breast. His mouth moved and Jenna's eyes widened. "I still don't think anything is happening."

I didn't know what to tell her. The two of them would surely figure it out. And if they didn't, maybe Allie would have some pointers she hadn't mentioned.

"That was really sweet of you," Jenna said. "You know, I got your back, too, okay?"

"I know," I said.

"I'm glad you're here with me, Joss." Tears started to roll down Jenna's cheeks. She didn't bother to wipe them away. "Dammit, I'm so emotional."

The smile that curled my lips surprised me. I placed my hand on Jenna's shoulder. "I'm glad we're together too."

"Get some sleep," Jenna said.

"Are you sure?" I asked. I still wasn't sure if I would be able to close my eyes.

"Yeah," Jenna said. "I just want to be with him."

I lingered.

"Go on," Jenna said. "I'll be okay."

"I like looking at him too," I said. After a few seconds, I forced myself to move my feet toward the stairs. "Wake me if you need me, okay?"

"Yeah, I will," Jenna said.

I yawned as I plodded up the stairs. It was crazy but I missed him already. Something told me I wouldn't get a lot of sleep before Jenna needed me.

I wasn't sure how long I'd been in bed when I heard Jenna's frustrated cries. The sky outside the window was dark and I'd forgotten to light the candle in the bedroom.

"What's going on?" I shouted seconds before I stubbed my toe.

Jenna groaned loudly. "He doesn't like me! He won't eat!"

20

ADAM

Eli slopped down a pile of what I assumed, and hoped, was oatmeal. He set down a bowl for Heather first. Once we all had our food, he held out his hands, resting them on the edge of the table.

"Let's give thanks to God for this bounty," Eli said. Leah and Heather took his hands, and then they took mine. "Dear Lord, we thank you for this wonderful meal and for keeping us safe during these trying and troubling times. Please continue to look out for us. Amen."

"Amen," Heather said quickly and enthusiastically.

"Amen," Leah and I murmured simultaneously.

Eli rubbed his hands together and grinned. "Good. Then let's eat."

The slop was delicious. Maybe it was because it was warm or maybe it was because it had a lot of cinnamon and sugar. I couldn't stop shoveling it into my mouth.

"So, Heather," Eli said setting down his spoon. He wasn't as ravenously hungry as the rest of us. "Tell me about your travels."

"It was awful. Dreadful, really," Heather said. "A nightmare I don't want to relive. I don't even know how long I'd been wandering around aimlessly before I ran into Leah and Adam. Then it only took us a short time to find you."

Eli clasped his hands together as he eyed Leah and me. "You've only been together for a short time then?"

"Um, yeah, but they saved my life," Heather said as her eyes darted around.

"Huh," Eli said. "So, you don't know them very well at all?"

The back of my neck felt hot. Eli's bushy brows blended together to make one long caterpillar stretching across his forehead.

"What if they're spies or thieves?" Eli asked Heather as if we weren't even there. "Maybe they're murderers."

"We're not any of those things," Leah replied.

Eli didn't turn away from Heather. "It's amazing you survived out there when you're so damn stupid."

"Hey," I said pressing my left hand down against the table.

"Uncle Eli," Heather said puffing out her bottom lip as she looked down at her lap. "They could have killed me but they didn't. They helped me."

"I don't want strangers nosing around my stuff," Eli said. "You should have known better than to bring them here."

Leah stood, the chair hissed against the floor as she pushed it back. "We'll leave then. Come on, Adam. Let's get our things."

"Sit down!" Eli said slamming his fist against the table. The bowls and spoons rattled noisily.

Leah dropped to her seat like a frightened child. Her expression, however, didn't show an ounce of fear. Her brows were angled with contained rage.

"My apologies," Eli said. "I'm not a trusting person, as you may have put together. Heather was careless but you're here now."

"We'll get out of your hair," Leah said. When she got up this time, she was much calmer. "We really didn't mean to impose."

We should have known better than to come this way. My lack of sleep led me to make poor choices.

Leah swayed to the side. She gripped the edge of the table but her eyes closed and she started to tip to the side.

I managed to get to her just before she passed out.

"Leah!" I said shaking her body gently. "Leah!"

She didn't open her eyes. I scooped her up and carried her to the bedroom. Her body felt so warm against mine.

After I set her down on the bed, I placed my lips on her forehead. She was burning up.

"Is she okay?" Heather asked from behind me.

I glanced at her standing in the doorway. "I don't know. She has a fever."

Leah groaned as she rolled onto her side. She pulled her knees to her stomach.

"I don't feel good," Leah moaned.

"What's wrong?" I asked sitting down on the bed next to her. I stroked her hair, brushing it away from her face.

"I'll get her some medicine," Heather said. "I'm sure I have something, or maybe Uncle Eli does."

Leah fell asleep even though Heather hadn't been gone long. She returned, holding a small cup.

"Here," Heather said handing it to me. "It's Uncle Eli's secret recipe."

I looked into the cup. There was a white powdery film on the surface of the water. Tiny bubbles floated up, creating a fine mist as they popped.

"What is this exactly?" I asked.

"Tummy medicine," Heather said with a shrug. "You know, that bubbly stuff. I think he adds a pinch of sugar and lemon juice."

I gently shook Leah until she opened her eyes. She didn't ask what I was helping her drink. She was too sick to care and that worried me.

"Uncle Eli said it'll fix her right up," Heather said. "It's a passed down family recipe. I remember my mom making it for me when I was little. It tastes terrible, even with the sugar but she'll feel better in the morning."

"I hope so," I said.

Heather left the room. I sat with Leah, staring at her as she rested uncomfortably.

Beads of sweat gathered at her temples and the back of her neck, yet she shivered. I pulled the blankets up, only to take them off her when she looked too warm.

I felt helpless. I didn't know what to do for her. I didn't know how to help her.

Useless.

The word repeated over and over again in the back of my mind. It wasn't my voice I heard, though… it was Eva's.

She haunted me. If I narrowed my eyes, I could see her standing in the corner of the room. Maybe that was why I couldn't sleep. It wasn't because I didn't feel safe, it was because Eve wouldn't let me.

When morning came, Leah wasn't doing any better and I hadn't gotten much sleep again. Every little movement she made woke me. I wanted to help but she'd whimper and fall back asleep.

"Leah," I said.

"Hmm?"

"Are you feeling any better?" I asked.

She shook her head.

"Do you want anything to eat?"

"No," she groaned.

"You should try to eat something," I said.

Leah turned away from me, pushing the blankets off her body. She started shivering.

A soft knock at the door made me look up. I didn't bother to get up.

"Yes?" I said loudly.

The door opened but Heather didn't come forward. "I just wanted to check on Leah. Hope that's okay."

"Yeah, of course," I said. "Come in."

Heather pressed her palms to her sides and entered the room. She had her bag over her shoulder.

"I'll get her more of my uncle's medicine but I was hoping I could take a look at her wound," Heather said.

"Sure," I said.

"I wonder if it might be infected," Heather said. "If so, I might have something that could help."

Leah kept still as Heather raised up her pants and

pulled back the bandage. Heather winced and covered her nose.

"Yeah," Heather said. "I'm pretty sure this is infected."

"Okay, so what do we do now?" I asked.

"I'm not exactly sure but I'll clean it and give her one of the antibiotics in my bag," Heather said. "Then we cross our fingers."

I licked my dry lips. "What if it doesn't work?"

"Let's just hope that it does," Heather said looking into my eyes.

The next three days were some of the worst days of my life. I was worried sick about what Leah was going through. I worried so much I couldn't eat. My stomach felt like a can of soda that had been shaken... bubbly and ready to explode.

Every day, Heather said the wound looked better. The redness diminished and Leah didn't seem as bothered when the bandages were changed.

Still, she didn't get better. In fact, she continued to get worse.

STEVIE

A group of eight men cheered as they cut me down. They weren't careful and I fell hard into the mud.

Mud covered half of my face and body. I looked up and they all laughed.

"Our mud-covered prize!" one of the men said.

A man leaned close and touched the tip of my nose. "Where did you come from, little mud bug?"

I bit my cheek to stop my eyes from rolling. Then I buried my hands into the mud to stop myself from throwing my fist into his face.

"She's an angel that fell from the sky," one of the other men joked.

I kept my head down but my eyes flashed upward at each one of the men. I was committing their faces to memory.

"Hey!" one of the men shouted before kicking me hard in the hip. "He asked you where you came from."

"From the north," I said scrunching up my nose as mud seeped into my mouth. The gritty bits crunched between my teeth.

"I doubt it," the guy replied grabbing my arm and roughly lifting me off the ground in one swift movement. "Let's get her to Zachary."

I dug my feet into the mud. "What if I don't want to meet Zachary?"

"You don't have a choice in the matter," the rough guy said.

"What's Zachary going to do?" I asked.

I wanted to jerk myself free but I knew it was pointless. I was going to be hauled to Zachary, whether I liked it or not.

"You'll find out soon enough," the guy grunted into my ear.

As they dragged me closer to the town, I glanced over my shoulder, hoping to catch a final glimpse of Shawn. There was a chance it was the last time I'd see him. I peered through the rain and mist but he wasn't anywhere to be seen, which made my lips curl slightly at the ends... he'd gotten away.

Shawn was going to be fine.

They led me to the poorly fenced in gated community. A black metal fence I could jump over lined the area. At the road, the gate was a bit taller and guarded by two men.

They smiled as they opened the gate. I felt like a perfectly cooked steak with how they were looking at me.

"What you got there?" one of them asked raising a brow.

"Mmm," the other said lightly touching his thumb to his bottom lip. He smirked as he looked me up and down.

Unable to stop myself, I swung my free arm. My closed fist connected with Mr. Smirk's cheek, causing my knuckles to crack.

His head jerked to the side but he didn't change his expression. If anything, it only made his smirk grow.

"I like it rough too," he whispered.

"Enough flirting, you too," the guy holding me said. He jerked me forward and led me down the road as the other guys dispersed.

I laughed. "You don't want backup?"

"Why would I need backup?" he said with a snort.

I twisted to the side sharply and yanked my arm free. As I ducked, I swung my leg out and threw my foot into the back of his knee.

He fell into the mud and I took off. My foot slipped behind me but I managed to maintain my balance. Unfortunately, I didn't make it far before I was tackled.

The guy grabbed my shirt and pulled me up. I saw his fist coming toward my face and I tried to get out of the way but he didn't let go of me.

The blow to my face was intensely painful. My brain started to numb. I tried to keep my eyes open but I couldn't.

Everything went black.

———

I groaned as I forced my eyes to open. My wrists were bound.

The room was dark except for a few battery-powered lanterns in the corners of the room. I was tied to a chair. There was a fireplace to my left and a window with the curtain drawn to the right.

Several shadows moved around the room. The man in the chair across from me cleared his throat.

In the dim light, I could see he was clean-shaven. His jaw was perfectly angled and his face sculpted. Something told me I was sitting across from Zachary. What I hadn't expected was how good looking he was.

"Are you all right, my dear?" he asked. His steepled fingertips tapped together. "My friends here can get a little rough."

"I'm fine," I said as I straightened my spine. My

outer shell was up and there was no way I was going to let anyone know how terrified I was.

Had Shawn gotten back to the compound? Did Gage know I'd been captured?

"I'm Zachary and this is my community," the guy said holding out his arms. "Let me be the first to welcome you."

"Um, thanks," I said.

Zachary smiled. "You're not happy to be out of the rain?"

"Of course, I am," I said unable to hide the sarcasm.

"What's your name?" Zachary asked leaning forward.

I hesitated. "Stevie."

"Is that the truth?" Zachary asked cocking his head.

"Why would I lie about my name?" I asked.

"You paused as if you didn't know your name."

I huffed. "I was punched in the face. Took me a second to remember."

"I'm sorry about that," Zachary said. "Can you tell me where are you from?"

"I was living in a small house to the north with my parents," I said. The lie came so quickly I almost believed it myself.

Zachary, however, shook his head. "We've checked every house for miles. No one lives to the north."

"Well, I did."

"What color was your house?"

"White."

Zachary cocked a brow. "We know about a group to the south."

"Oh?"

"Know anything about that?"

"Nope. Wish I did since things have been rough for me since my parents died," I said.

Zachary pressed his lips together. "Sorry to hear that. You don't seem all that upset."

"You must have forgotten that one of your goons punched me in the face. Forgive me if I'm still in a bad mood about it," I said sharply.

"Well," Zachary said as he got out of his wooden chair. "Since you have nothing to go back to, this should be easy."

My eyes narrowed as I bit down on my cheek. I breathed into my nose to keep myself calm.

"We'd like it if you joined us," Zachary said with a laugh.

"That's all?" I managed to ask.

"That's all. We'll take good care of you here. Keep you fed and dry," Zachary said.

I licked my dry lips, tasting mud that had managed

to stay on even after walking through the rain. "And if I don't want to stay."

"Why wouldn't you want to stay?" Zachary asked. "You have nowhere to go and we'll take care of you."

"I haven't liked what I've seen so far," I said flatly.

"Are we still on the getting hit thing?" Zachary asked.

I gave him a quick nod.

"He'll be reprimanded," Zachary said crossing his heart with his finger. "You have my word."

"I don't want to stay here," I said even though I knew there was zero percent chance he was going to let me go. If there had been any chance of that, they wouldn't have gone to all the trouble they had just to catch me.

Zachary sighed. "Take her to building six. Let her think about her options."

"What are my options?" I asked trying to wiggle free from my restraints.

"If you want, you can choose to stay peacefully or if you can choose to be difficult," Zachary said.

I laughed. "I can answer that now. It's not going to be peacefully."

Zachary jerked his chin toward the door. All hints of a smile disappeared from his face.

Two of his men walked toward me. One of them

bent down and cut the rope around my middle. My body was free but my wrists were still tied.

They worked together to lift me out of the chair and drag me through the house. The rain cooled my hot cheeks as it washed down over me, taking what remained of the mud with it.

"Let me go," I said softly. "You both know this is wrong."

They ignored me. It was as though they'd heard it before and were numb to my pleas.

I could still see the house I'd been in with Zachary when we stepped up to a blue, two-story house. The man on my right reached into his pocket and pulled out a key. He opened the door and roughly pushed me inside.

I landed hard. My face smacking into the wood floorboards stunned me. I growled as a knee pressed into my back but felt a bit of relief when my hands were freed. Seconds later, the pressure released and the door closed behind me.

I got to my feet and placed my hands on the door. My hand gripped the knob as I angrily attempted to twist it. Unsurprisingly, it didn't budge.

I took several steps back, clenching my shaking hands into tight fists. My eyes shifted toward the window. There were thick bars bolted to the outside of the house.

I was essentially in a prison. There was no way out.

A hand touched my shoulder and I gasped as I pulled away.

"Sorry!" a woman said as she held up her hands. "The new ones always react the same, yet I keep trying to do that."

"What?" I said shaking my head.

The woman talking to me wasn't the only one there. Five other women stepped out of the shadows, looking at me with sorrow filling their eyes.

"Poor girl," an older woman with gray hair said shaking her head.

Two of the others hugged each other. They looked at me as if they were afraid I might lunge at them at any second.

The one closest to me offered me a sympathetic smile. "It's confusing, I know."

"What's going on here?" I asked.

"Welcome to hell," a second girl said as she walked over to the window. Her black hair fell over her dark eyes.

"I'm Melinda," the girl who was still holding up her hands said. Her head tipped to the side, indicating the girl at the window. "That's Lydia. Those two are Tami and Abigail and—"

"I'm Mrs. Cottonwood," the gray-haired woman

said stretching out her thin hand. "But you can call me Ida."

I swallowed before shaking her hand. "Hi, I'm Stevie."

"Nice to meet you, dear," she said with a small curtsy. "It's unfortunate that it's under these circumstances."

"You can say that again," I mumbled. "What is this place? Why are you locked up?"

"All of the women are locked up," Tami said.

I shook my head. "How many women are locked up? Is it just us?"

"Oh, definitely not," Melinda said. "If I had to guess, I'd say there are maybe twenty of us?"

"Hell, no," Lydia said. "There are at least forty women here. All of us are treated like shit. We're maids and waitresses. Slaves and whores."

Ida clapped her hands together. "Lydia! Watch your mouth."

"I'm not wrong." Lydia shrugged. She lifted her shirt and turned. There were dark purple bruises scattered on her skin. "We're also punching bags."

I touched my face. "I've already experienced that."

"Sorry to hear that," Melinda said with a frown. "The women here are not treated well. We can't leave unless we're called to do a job. We're under constant watch. If we speak, we're slapped and if we try to escape, we're killed."

"How did you even end up here?" Lydia asked.

"I need to get to the pharmacy," I said. "One of the people in my group desperately needs his medication."

Lydia cocked her head to the side. "The people in your group? You look like you're all alone to me, girl."

It was probably a mistake but I couldn't stop myself. I told the defeated looking women everything about the compound.

It wasn't like the men running the place didn't know about it. The only thing they didn't know was that I had come from there. Although, I was almost positive they suspected it.

Their eyes widened and their mouths dropped open. They stared at me as they tried to decide if I was telling the truth.

"Now, where is the pharmacy and what is the quickest way to get there?" I asked. I looked at them one by one as I exhaled slowly.

Lydia crossed her arms. "I can get you out."

2 2

―――――

JOSS

Jenna was frustrated. When Cal cried, she'd hand him to Allie or me, claiming he didn't like her.

"He doesn't get that I've just given birth," Jenna complained.

"He probably didn't enjoy the experience that much either," I said.

Jenna shot me a look that almost knocked me back. I looked down at Cal to avoid her deadly glare.

"Sorry," I muttered.

"I just don't know what I'm going to do if he won't eat," Jenna said. "He tries and tries but nothing comes out. It's not like I can give a newborn oatmeal."

"It'll take a bit for your milk to come in," Allie said. "At least, I think that's what they said."

Jenna crossed her arms and grimaced as if it were painful. "And meanwhile he starves to death? How

153

long can he wait? What if I can't make milk because of how malnourished we are?"

"I'll go out and try to find formula," I said. "There must be some somewhere, right? I can't imagine that would be an item that's in very high demand right now."

"You know I can't ask you to do that," Jenna said.

"You didn't ask," I said. "It might just be what I have to do."

Cal started crying. His sharp little cry pierced my ears like tiny daggers stabbing at the side of my brain.

"Anyone in a few miles will hear him," Jenna said taking him back. She bounced up and down until Cal cried himself back to sleep. "It might be time for all of us to strike out. We need help."

"There's nothing out there," Allie said.

"There has to be," Jenna said without looking up. "There just has to be for all our sakes."

A half-hour later, when Cal woke up crying again, Jenna sat down on the sofa and tried to feed him. Again, it just ended with more crying... from both of them and Jenna frustrated.

"Maybe it's time we talk about packing up what we have left and leaving," I said.

"Oh, yeah, he's more likely to eat in the cold rain," Jenna snapped. "We're just supposed to take turns carrying him? What if this house is all that's left?"

"I just don't want to end up back where I started," Allie said.

I shook my head. "None of us want to end up there."

"Cal could get sick," Jenna said.

"We'll bundle him up," I said. "Make a sling. It's not like we have that long left here anyway."

"What about all the bear meat?" Jenna asked.

Allie sighed. "There wasn't that much. He was a thin bear."

"We can take what we have," I said. "Besides, it's not like we can just live on bear meat forever."

Jenna placed a bundled Cal on a sheet on the floor. There were pillows around his sides, forming a little nest for him.

"Are you sure about this?" Jenna asked her voice much calmer.

"If you think it's better, I could go myself," I said.

"I really don't think we should separate," Jenna said.

I let out a breath. "I think it might be better if we head out while we have the energy. If we wait too long, it might just make everything harder."

"What if we don't find anything like this again?" Jenna asked.

"And what if we find something better?" I asked.

Jenna snorted. "Look at you looking for the bright

side of things. Sorry, Joss, there is no bright side anymore."

"I know that," I said. "But they'd want us to keep trying."

"Okay," Jenna said. "You're probably right but for the record, I don't think there will be anything better than this."

Cal started crying. Jenna covered her face.

"Aren't they supposed to sleep more than fifteen minutes at a time?" she asked.

"Want me to get him?" I asked.

Jenna held up her hand. "Nah. I might as well try to feed him again."

"I'll start packing our things," I said.

"Can I help?" Allie asked.

"Yeah, of course," I said.

We'd gathered as many bags as we could find in the house and start sorting and packing. Allie was kneeling on the floor, going through some of the packages. She stopped abruptly and placed her hands on her thighs.

"Joss?" She looked up at me. "Can I join you?"

"I just assumed you were coming with us," I said feeling the confusion wrinkle my eyebrows.

"Oh, good." She turned back to the bag. "I'm really worried about running into them again but I think I'm more afraid of being alone."

Whispers from the living room drifted through the air. My eyes narrowed, unable to decipher the words.

"I'll be right back," I said as I turned the corner into the living room.

Jenna was beaming as she pointed at Cal. Her voice was feather-soft. "It's working!"

"That's great," I said smiling at them.

"How's the packing going?" Jenna asked.

"There isn't much," I said crossing my arms. "We'll be ready to leave in the morning. If you're able."

Jenna stared at Cal with so much love in her eyes. "Yeah. I feel good."

"You're sure?" I asked.

"Positive. No pain. Nothing," Jenna said. "I feel really good. Better than I did when I was pregnant, to be honest."

Jenna yawned. She flicked her eyes toward me.

"Although I am tired," she said.

"I bet he'll sleep better with a full belly," I said.

"God, I hope so."

———

By the time morning came, we were ready to go. I hadn't slept well. I was anxious and worried that I was making a mistake.

Clover paced nervously at our feet. It was like she

knew what was happening and she wasn't thrilled about it.

Allie and I carried the two large backpacks and Jenna carried Cal in the sling we'd made for her. He looked so peaceful. It was too bad the rest of us couldn't feel the same way.

Jenna groaned when she was hit by the first raindrop. She turned and started back toward the house. Clover followed her.

"I quit," she said throwing a hand into the air.

"Jenna!" I said.

She turned back—her shoulders slumped. "If we don't find anything in a few days, we're coming back here, right?"

"Sure," I said. "But that won't make any sense since there isn't anything left to eat here."

"That's fine. I just don't want to die in the mud and rain," Jenna said.

We headed south like Robby had suggested. Our long break was over and it was time to get back to the plan.

Maybe things would get warmer as we traveled further south. Maybe the rain would stop. Of course, I didn't think it would.

"I hate this," Allie muttered.

"I know," Jenna said. "The rain is awful."

"That's not what I mean, but I don't like being wet either," Allie said.

I glanced at Allie over my shoulder. "What did you mean?"

"I hate being out in the open like this," Allie said her eyes darting in every direction. "It just feels like they're watching us."

"We'll see them," I said. There wasn't much around us other than a few dead trees and random shrubs. Everything was dying or already dead.

We spent most of the day walking. For the first several miles, we traveled quickly, stopping only to snack and for Jenna to feed Cal. The last few miles didn't go as well as they had at the start of our day.

None of us were used to walking so much. Eventually, a house came into view.

"We can stop there for the night," I said.

"What makes you think it's available?" Jenna asked.

I pressed my lips together and pulled the empty gun out of the back of my waistband. "I guess we'll find out."

"What do you plan to do with an empty gun?" Jenna asked snickering.

"No one else knows it's empty," I said keeping my eyes forward.

"Well, good luck with that," Jenna said. She was

becoming more and more like herself with every passing hour.

We approached the house cautiously. I peeked into the windows before stopping at the front door. Allie grabbed my hand as I reached for the handle.

"Aren't you going to knock?" she asked.

"Um, no?" I replied.

"If you do, maybe you'll hear someone moving inside. Then we can run," Allie said.

I hesitated. "Or maybe they'll get into a hiding place and ambush us."

"For the love of God," Jenna said pushing past me. She reached out and opened the door.

The hinges squeaked and whistled. If anyone would have been inside, they likely would have locked the door. Then again, maybe they'd forgotten just like Jenna had. In our case, we were lucky it had only been Allie and not someone dangerous.

"What is that god awful smell?" Jenna asked.

"Rotten food?" I said pinching my nose.

Allie leaned back, closing the door behind us. "That's not what rotten food smells like."

"What is it then?" Jenna asked.

"That's the smell of death," Allie said. She pulled on my arm, jerking me back. "Maybe we should leave. I think we should leave."

"You guys wait here," I said gripping the gun tighter.

Jenna clicked her tongue. "Hell no. We're staying together."

"Fine," I said. "Then follow me."

I hated that it felt like I was putting Cal in danger. I didn't know what else I could do. It was impossible to keep him safe while looking for somewhere for us to stay.

Our shoulders bumped together as we moved through the house. The smell became worse as we worked our way down the hallway toward the bedroom.

"I don't want to go in there," Allie whispered.

I opened the door and held my hand up to keep them back. The room was empty except for what was left of the body on the bed.

"Oh my God," I said covering my nose and mouth. "Back up! Back up!"

There was a hole in the middle of what I thought was a guy's forehead. The smell was sickening... strong enough, I felt light-headed.

I stepped back out into the hall and closed the door. The putrid scent wafted by before diminishing slightly.

"This isn't good," Allie said walking quickly back toward the living room.

"I don't think anyone is going to come back for him," I said. "Looks like he's been there a while."

"No, no, no," Allie said pacing. "It's one of them. One of the guys. They all wear those bulletproof vests."

The truth was, I hadn't noticed the vest. I believed her, though. I wasn't about to go back to verify her claim.

"They're everywhere!" Allie said. She balled her hands into tight fists and pressed them to the sides of her head. "They're going to find me! I won't go back! They won't make me go back!"

"Allie," I said speaking calmly. "No one is here. We're not going to let anyone take you."

Allie laughed hysterically. "There isn't anything you will be able to do to stop them. We have to leave!"

"He's dead," Jenna said. "Unless he comes back to life, which is ridiculous, there isn't anything he can do to you."

"I'm not worried about him," Allie growled. "It's the ones that are still living I'm worried about. You don't understand how awful they are. I'll die before I have to go back to them."

Allie whipped out a knife from her backpack. Her hand shook as she raised it to her throat.

I took a step toward her and she pressed the blade

into the skin. A drop of blood leaked out of the small cut she'd made.

Allie's chest was rising and falling rapidly. "Stay back. I'm going to do it and if you know what's good for you, you'll do it too."

23

—————

ADAM

Heather continued to bring Eli's concoction to Leah, even though it didn't seem to help. She'd bring me food and drink but I never could take in much of it.

When she was awake, Leah would complain of headaches. If I tried to get her to eat, she'd vomit.

Leah would push me away, just wanting to lay down.

"You'll feel better if you eat more. If you sit up," I said even though I didn't know what the hell I was talking about. I just so desperately wanted Leah to come back to me. "Take another drink."

Leah slapped my hand but it was less painful than a mosquito bite. She placed her hands on her stomach and groaned.

"I think I'm going to throw up again," Leah said.

164

I grabbed the bucket and held her up and she dry heaved three times before releasing a small amount of thick liquid. My heart pounded when I saw the blood on her lip.

She looked at me, her eyes barely open. "I think I'm done."

"Okay," I said afraid to look in the bucket. But I had to know.

I took in a breath and looked at the bottom. There wasn't much, but it was there. Blood.

I wiped the blood off her lip and rested a damp cloth on her forehead. "I'll be right back, okay?"

She gave me a slow nod and stared at the window. "Has it stopped raining yet?"

"No. It hasn't."

"Darn," she said before drifting off.

I quietly left the room even though I hated leaving her even for a second. Eli was standing at the window and Heather was at the table with her head buried in a thick book.

"Heard she's not doing well," Eli said without turning.

"It's bizarre," I said. "She's getting worse. I don't know what to do for her."

"Maybe she caught something out there," Eli said. "Happens more than you'd think."

My eyes narrowed. "It does? How do you know?"

"Those people that passed through here early on," Eli said shooting me a quick glance. "All of them were sick in one way or another. Some physically... some in the head."

"I see," I said.

"People always wanted what I had," Eli said turning halfway. "Part of the reason I moved out here in the first place. Much better out here where you don't have to deal with anyone."

The back of my neck prickled as if I'd backed into a cactus. "Sorry to hear that. I need to get some fresh air."

"Are you sure you want to go out there?" Eli asked his nose wrinkling. "Makes a mess."

"I'll be careful and I'm happy to clean up after myself," I said. "I haven't been feeling great myself and really could use the fresh air."

Eli stomped toward the kitchen. "If you must."

I rolled my eyes after I opened the door and stepped out. I stayed under the overhang for a long time, worried about pissing off Eli but I needed to move my legs.

I walked to the side of the house, away from the windows. I weaved between the trees, stopping when I nearly tripped over a large rock.

"What the...?"

There were five other similar rocks, each spaced

out the same distance from each other. It was almost perfect how far apart they were. There was no way they had just naturally been in those spots... someone had placed them there.

My stomach tightened. I wasn't sure if I was going to need to use the bathroom or if I was going to throw up.

I left the strange stones and made my way back to the house. Thankfully, by the time I got back, my stomach had settled, although there were lingering pains.

Maybe Eli was right. Maybe we were just coming down with something. That would probably be better than Leah having an infection, considering there were no doctors around.

I quickly cleaned up and changed into dry clothes. Leah watched me through narrowed slits as I moved around the room.

"Am I dreaming?" she asked.

"No, you're awake," I said.

"I feel so terrible," Leah said. "Where were you just now? I called for you."

I looked down at my bare feet. "I went out for a walk."

"A walk? Is it still raining?" she asked.

"Yeah," I said scrunching up my nose. "It's still raining."

"Why would you want to get wet?"

I sighed heavily. "I just wanted some fresh air. Felt a little claustrophobic in this house."

"I'm sorry I'm sick," Leah said.

The bed squeaked as I lowered myself down next to her. "Don't worry about it. Just work on getting better, okay?"

"I will," she said giving me a weak smile.

I reached down to wrap my arm around her shoulder but hesitated when I saw the strands of hair on the pillow. It wasn't much but her hair had fallen out.

My heart raced as terror pumped through my veins. What was happening to her?

I left it where it was because I couldn't tell her. I pressed my lips to her forehead.

"I love you, Leah," I said. "You know that, right?"

"Yeah," she said. "I know that."

"What about me?" I asked softly.

Her lip curled just a smidge. "What about you?"

"Tell me," I said. Or rather, I begged.

"Of course, I do," she said with her eyes closed.

Several hours later, Heather brought in some food. Leah didn't take more than a few sips but I ate ravenously. I hadn't felt like eat but my body wanted the fuel so that I could be there for Leah.

"Let me check her wound," Heather said. "Did she take her antibiotic?"

"Yes," I said. "But she hasn't eaten anything."

"It looks better," Heather said. "That's strange, isn't it?"

I nodded as I leaned forward to take a look. "Huh."

It was still a nasty cut but it wasn't as red and the pus had cleared up substantially. Some sections had scabbed over and actually looked as though they were beginning to heal.

"I guess it's working but just not helping her yet," Heather said. She looked up at me and smiled. "Maybe that's good news. It could be a sign that she'll get back to her old self again soon."

"I hope you're right," I said.

Heather hadn't even left the room before I started to experience stomach cramps again. It seemed as though something I was eating didn't agree with me but I wasn't sure what it could have been.

Eli hadn't been serving me anything that unusual. It wasn't like oatmeal, canned beans, and mashed potatoes would cause my stomach to hurt.

I pressed my hands to my stomach. Heather's eyes filled with concern.

"Are you okay?" she asked.

"It's my stomach," I said.

"I should get you some of Eli's stomach medicine," Heather said.

I shook my head. "Nah, I think I'll just wait it out. I think I'm just adjusting to eating a little different from how I had been."

It really wasn't all that much different. The only difference was that Eli was serving us food that was warmed up.

"Maybe but I'm fine," Heather said.

I smiled at her. "That's good. I'm sure I'll be fine too. I've probably just been eating too much."

"We've all been eating the same amount," Heather said. "Uncle Eli uses a food scale to weigh out our portions."

"Wow," I said. "That's taking it to a new level."

Heather giggled. "That's Uncle Eli for you."

"I think I'm going to rest for a bit," I said lowering myself down on the bed. "Wait for this to pass."

"Okay," Heather said. "If you need anything, just let me know, okay?"

"Sure thing," I said.

I listened as she took her bag and collected the food. The door clicked as she closed it behind her.

I stared at the wall.

Leah's infection was improving but she was getting worse. It was so bad that her hair was falling out and she was puking up blood.

Whatever was making her sick didn't seem like it was from the infection and it didn't seem like it was a virus. I wasn't even sure if there was a virus that made you vomit blood and lose your hair.

There was something else going on and I was determined to find out what it was. Hours later, when it was dark and I was sure everyone was asleep, I took a candle. It was time to have a look around.

STEVIE

I t was pitch black when Lydia brought me to the second floor. She studied me. "You're sure about this? Once you're out there, I can't get you back in."

"I'm positive," I said.

Lydia looked out the window before she slid it open. "The idiots didn't bolt this one down."

She moved the bars, making a small opening between the metal and the house. "I don't know if I'll fit."

"I did," Lydia said looking at me. "You're not that much bigger. Perhaps you are telling the truth about your place."

"I am," I said.

"Will you go there after you get the medicine?" Lydia asked.

My lips pressed together. "Yeah. I have to get back to the man who needs the medicine."

"Right," she said unable to hide her disappointment. She forced a smile. "Well, if you ever think of a way to help us, we'll all still be here."

"I'll talk to everyone," I said. "We won't leave you here."

Lydia looked at her feet, chuckling. Her eyes shifted up.

"I'm not a fool. I know I won't see you again," she said.

"Come with me," I said. "You can show me to the pharmacy and I'll take you back to my place."

Lydia blinked several times as she considered my proposition. "I don't think you'll make it more than a few blocks before they find you and kill you."

"They didn't kill you," I said raising a brow.

"If I'm caught again, they most certainly will," Lydia said.

"Okay," I said sticking my feet out of the window.

Lydia reached forward and grabbed my hand. "Be careful where you step. It's like walking on mushrooms."

"I will," I said lowering myself down. The metal bars scraped along my back but somehow, I squeezed through the tight space.

I let go of Lydia's hand and grabbed onto a brick

that stuck out from the side of the house. It was like pieces of the house had shifted around.

"Oh, screw it," Lydia said as she started to climb out of the window. "I'd rather be dead than stuck in this building another day."

The darkness and rain kept us hidden. Some of the houses had a glowing lantern under the overhang at the front door but the light didn't stretch far. It was easy for us to stay hidden but it was a challenge to navigate our way through the streets.

We couldn't see more than a few feet in front of us and the closer we got to town, the harder it was to find our way through the streets. I covered my laugh when I walked into a mailbox that somehow managed to blend in with the surrounding darkness.

"What's so funny?" Lydia asked.

"Nothing," I said keeping my hands out in front of me. "Just walking into things."

"Well, be careful," Lydia cautioned.

"I'm trying."

Lydia turned, stopping in front of a building that was nestled between two other shops. The front had once been mostly glass but it was now sprinkled in pieces on the ground.

"How the hell am I going to see what I need?" I asked as I ducked inside the building. It was even darker inside.

"They usually keep candles in here just in case," Lydia said. "Hopefully, they keep matches in here too."

"That would be nice."

Lydia's eyes glowed in the darkness. "We have to be careful though, they could see the light. One candle. That's it."

"Right," I said.

"If I can even find—ah-ha! Here it is," Lydia said stepping behind the front desk.

I could hear her flicking a lighter in the darkness. My eyes darted around as I waited for the flame.

"These things can be stubborn," Lydia said clicking nervously.

"Can I try?" I asked.

"Sure, but it's no use," she said handing me the lighter. She crossed her arms as she watched me struggle for several minutes. "Told you."

I drew in a breath and flicked the wheel again. The flame was low but it was there.

"Ha!" I said gesturing for the candle.

Lydia held it in her shaking hand. It lit almost instantly, giving off a dim glow. Our shadows dancing on the walls.

"Hurry," she said. "What are we looking for?"

I pulled the piece of paper out of my back pocket and showed it to her. We walked through the already open door and into the back where the medicine was stored. The shelves were missing items but they weren't bare.

White and amber bottles were scattered on the counters and on the floor. There was no organization, at least nothing that I could make sense of.

"We're never going to find it," Lydia said.

"Keep looking," I urged before I climbed up on the counter.

"Be careful," Lydia said. "I don't want you to fall."

"That makes two of us." My finger moved along the names of the drugs printed on the labels. It was like trying to read a bowl of alphabet soup.

Until... I saw it.

I snatched the bottled and shoved it into my pocket before hopping down off the counter. I blew out the candle.

"Did you find it?" Lydia's voice was soft and hopeful, touched with surprise.

"I think so. As long as no one messed with what was inside," I said.

"Let's get out of here then," Lydia said with a hop. "I can't believe this. I can't believe I might actually get out of here."

I smiled but she likely couldn't see it in the dark. "Which way?"

She tapped her finger to her lips and led me down

the street. Our feet splashed through the puddles as we moved as quickly as possible through the night.

The glow from the lanterns at the houses were to our left and grew fainter with each step. Lydia stopped abruptly and I slammed into her back, nearly knocking her down.

"What the hell, Lydia?" I said sucking in a breath.

"Should have guessed that was you," a deep-voiced boomed as a beam of light was slapped on Lydia's face.

"It's not what you think," Lydia said waving her hands.

The light flashed to me. "Who's this?"

"No one," I replied.

"Must be the new girl," another man's voice said. I hadn't seen anyone else standing there except for the man holding the flashlight.

There were probably others that I couldn't see but that didn't stop me. I dipped to the side out of the light and dashed away into the shadows.

The light danced around. I jumped and ducked but the light was faster and so was the man chasing me.

He grabbed my arm and jerked me to a stop. "You're going to be punished for this."

I swung but he anticipated my move. He ducked and laughed. His fingertips dug into my arm.

"I know all about you," he whispered. "We've all

been warned you like to fight back. Won't be long until they beat that out of you."

My jaw tensed. I loosened the instant I saw the fear in Lydia's eyes.

"This was my idea," I said. "Let her go."

"That's not how this works," the guy said.

Without another word, we were whisked back to the houses. We weren't brought to the house we'd been locked up in. We were brought to Zachary's house.

They didn't say much. Zachary sat in a soft, tall-backed chair with his arms crossed.

"I'm very disappointed in you both," he said. It was the only full sentence I could recall having heard before the beatings started.

I bit my cheek as I was smacked around. There were words but they faded in and out. I wasn't even sure if I'd heard them.

Obedience.

Rules.

Consequences.

I was flat on the floor with my cheek pressed against the floorboards when Lydia crashed down next to me. Her eyes were wide open.

She stared at me. Her lips moved but only for a second before the life left her.

Lydia was gone. And even though I tried not to... I cried.

I was beaten. Broken.

There were cuts on my skin that burned. Bruises that were so deep it felt as though they'd never heal.

It took two of them to drag me back to my prison house, not because I fought back but because I wouldn't even get to my feet. They were forced to carry me.

I kept my eyes closed until I heard the door lock. The others looked at me with concern and worry.

"Where's Lydia?" Melinda asked.

"It's my fault," I mumbled.

"What's your fault?" Tami asked holding onto Abigail.

I sniffed so hard it felt like something was stabbing my brain. "She's dead. They beat us. They went too far."

"That's not your fault," Melinda said as rage filled her eyes.

"She wouldn't have left if it hadn't been for me," I said.

Melinda took my hand into hers and I winced. "It was her choice to go. You didn't force her."

"I told her we'd get out of here," I said. "I failed her in so many ways. It's my fault."

"You tried to help her," Lydia said. She was only trying to make me feel better.

I pulled my hand away and painfully rolled on my

other side, turning my back to all of them. It was over. I'd lost.

There wasn't anything left I could and there was no way I was going to risk losing anyone else. I'd done enough damage.

I guess it had worked. They beat everything I was out of me. They'd won.

JOSS

I held up both hands. "Allie. Calm down. We'll leave, okay? We don't have to stay here. If you want to leave, we'll leave."

Allie stared at me as if trying to make sense of my words. After a long moment, she let her hand fall to her side. The knife clanked when it hit the floor.

She drew in a breath and picked it up, quickly tucking it into the bag as if she were trying to hide it.

"I'm sorry," she said bursting into tears. Allie crouched down, sobbing as she hugged her knees. "I'm so sorry. I'm such a mess."

Cal started crying. Either he was hungry again or Allie's outburst had frightened him. Maybe, and there was a good chance, it was both.

"It's okay," I said. "Just a quick break so Jenna can feed Cal. Is that okay?"

Allie sucked in a breath and nodded. "It's okay. I'm fine now. I panicked. It happens sometimes now. I never had these attacks before but I get them now."

"That smell will kill us. We can't stay here anyway," Jenna said taking a seat on the sofa. Cal was calmly having his feast. He couldn't have cared less about our surroundings.

We checked for food but the place had been cleared out. We each had a quick snack and some water from our bags before we headed back out into the rain. I worried that we wouldn't find another place to stop before nightfall. And by the way Jenna's eyes moved around, I knew she was thinking the same thing.

What I really wanted, more than anything, was to find another house we could stay safely inside for a long time. Something with lots of food. And something far away from other places. A place where we'd be safe.

Of course, I wasn't foolish enough to believe that a safe place existed. We were walking to our graves and I think on some level, we all knew it.

Maybe we were all ready in our own way. I was almost certain I was.

I missed Robby fiercely. It wasn't the same without him. It wasn't the same without Caleb either. Sure, I was with Jenna and Allie too, but that didn't help me feel any less empty.

We'd walked for miles. Our pace, slow and defeated.

In the distance, there was what appeared to be the remains of a gas station. It wouldn't be the safest place to stop but it would have to suffice.

I peeked into the cracked glass of the front window before we entered. The bell connected to the door jingled loudly.

"Geez," I said pressing my palm to my chest.

I sniffed the air as though I was expecting the mind-numbing scent of the dead but all I smelled was the faint odor of overcooked hot dogs. It was either my imagination or the smell was ingrained into the walls.

"Let's check for food," I said. "We won't be able to heat anything up here but pack it in the hopes we can at some point in the near future. We need to keep everything we find that could be of use."

"We know, Joss," Jenna said.

There were a few items on the shelves but nothing significant. Jenna started clapping her hands.

"You guys! Look at this!" Jenna squealed.

I ran to her, hoping to see a fresh cheeseburger and a large side of fries. Instead, there was a box of baby wipes and a small bag of diapers.

"I struck gold!" Jenna clapped her hands again.

"We don't have room for that entire box of wipes," I said.

"I know," Jenna said. "What we can't take, we use. We can clean up. A baby wipes bath."

I opened my mouth but snapped it shut. "That's not a bad idea."

"We'll take turns in the bathroom," Jenna said. "I'll go first because I found them."

"It's not going to last," I said. "That gross, dusty, sticky feeling will be back the second we step back out into the rain."

"Still, it will be nice while it lasts," Jenna said with a shrug.

The bell over the door jingled and we all turned. A man with a black vest stepped into the gas station and closed the door behind him.

"What's this about?" he asked. His eyes darted for a second toward the door behind the counter. "Terrance?"

The door popped open and another guy stepped out. He covered his yawn.

"Sorry, Randy. Ned and Vince fell asleep," Terrance said.

"Seems as though maybe you did too," Randy said jerking his thumb toward us. "We have visitors."

"Whoa-ho-ho!" Terrance said as he waddled around the front counter. "They look young."

I dared a quick glance at Allie. Her breaths were coming quickly. She was frozen with fear.

I pulled the knife out of her backpack and held it out in front of us. The muscles in my jaw were stiff and tight. Painful.

"Stay back," I said.

Jenna and Allie were behind me. There was no other way out besides the front door. Unless, of course, there was a way to break the glass of the cracked front window.

There was no doubt in my mind that the men in front of us were some of the men that Allie had warned us about. I didn't like the way the two guys were looking at us.

But then it wasn't just us they were looking at. It was something even more terrifying. They were eyeing Cal.

The guy in front, Randy, pulled a gun. "Get the other two."

"Ned, Vince, get out here," Terrance called. "Randy's back."

"That's not what I meant," Randy muttered.

Terrance shrugged as the other two came out. They stretched and yawned but their eyes widened when they spotted us.

"You brought us back a treat?" Ned asked with a laugh.

Randy grimaced. "They were already here when I

arrived. You idiots had one job and you blew it. Boss isn't going to be happy to hear about this."

"He won't care when he sees what we bring back for him," Ned said. "Three more helpers and a baby. We've found the needle in the haystack."

"Three needles," the one they'd called Vince said with a laugh.

Allie started screaming. "I won't go back! I won't! I'd rather die.

"That can be arranged," Randy said stomping forward.

I swung the knife but missed. Randy pushed me aside, knocking both Allie and me over like a pair of dominoes.

He grabbed Jenna and pulled her away from us. She kicked and punched at him with her free hand.

"Let me go, asshole!" Jenna shouted. "You'll hurt my baby!"

Ned reached toward her and peeled Cal away from her. Jenna opened her mouth and released her pain with a scream.

"Nooooo!" she threw her tightly closed fists at Randy as she squirmed to break free. "Give him back! You'll hurt him!"

Tears burned the back of my eyeballs. I thought my knees were going to give out but they didn't. Adrenaline surged through my veins. I lunged forward, slicing Randy's arm with the sharp edge of the knife.

"Jesus," he said turning to look at his arm. He didn't let go of Jenna, even though blood poured out of his forearm. "Get her! And the other one too!"

"No, no, no," Allie shouted as she covered her ears and kicked her legs.

Before Terrance could get to me, I swung the knife at Randy again. I cut the same arm again... this time, the back of his hand. He dropped his gun to the floor.

Allie scrambled forward and picked it up. She didn't hesitate to stand and shoot.

Randy touched his neck. His body vibrated and he let go of Jenna.

"You bitch," he said. He took a step and dropped heavily to the ground.

"Randy!" Terrance yelled before a shot rang out.

My eyes darted around, making sure Allie and Jenna were both fine. Cal was still in Ned's arms.

He'd missed.

Allie sucked in a sharp breath. She turned slightly, firing the gun again.

Terrance gurgled nonsense before blood dripped out of his mouth. He took a step back into the wall and slumped down to the floor. His head was tilted and his eyes blankly stared forward.

Vince raised his gun. His hands were shaking wildly.

"Shoot them!" Ned said.

"I can't! They're just... they're just kids. I can't do it," he said shaking his head.

Ned swallowed hard. "You know what the boss will do if you don't."

"I know," Vince said. He turned the gun on himself and pulled the trigger. Blood sprinkled out, splattering the wall behind him.

Ned clutched Cal to his chest and charged forward. He pushed Jenna with his palm, just above the center of his chest.

She fell to the ground, cracking her head against the bottom of one of the shelves. Her eyes rolled back in her head.

The bell above the door jingled. Allie kept trying to fire but the gun was empty.

Ned was getting away with Cal.

ADAM

I felt uncomfortable creeping through the house. I wasn't entirely sure what I was doing or what I was even looking for.

There wasn't anything unusual in the living room, dining room, or in the bathroom. The kitchen was the last room to go through unless, of course, I wanted to make my way to the bunker.

I opened the first cupboard and then the second. All that was inside were plates, bowls, and some plastic storage containers. Everything was neatly organized. The next had the cups, glasses, and mugs.

It was an ordinary kitchen that was until I got to the last cupboard door. The hinge squealed as I pulled it open. I froze in place, worried the sound had been too loud.

My body was stiff as I listened for sounds of

someone coming but there wasn't anything except for the rain hitting the roof and windows.

Inside the cupboard was a locked metal box. But there was no key nearby that I could see.

I opened the drawers one by one, desperately searching for the key. Each one was perfectly organized and none of them contained a key or even anything I could use to attempt to pick open the lock. Not that I would even know how to do such a thing.

My fingers gripped the edge of the counter. I pressed my hands to my face, muffling my groan.

The locked box was likely where Eli stored his valuables. With how paranoid he seemed, a locked box didn't seem that out of place. That didn't stop me from wanting to know what was inside.

Unfortunately, I wasn't going to find out. I grabbed the candle and headed back to the bedroom.

I stopped when I saw Eli's jacket hanging on the hook at the front door. My eyes glanced toward his room. It was just me, the rain, and his jacket.

I placed each step carefully. The rough feel of the fabric of his coat felt scratchy against my hand.

I hesitated when I felt the metal against my fingertips. The acrid taste at the back of my throat threatened to choke me.

My hand squeezed around the keys as I slowly pulled them from Eli's coat pocket. There were several different keys on the ring but of course, there was a chance none of them would open the metal box.

It was like something had control over me as I walked back to the kitchen. My eyes were focused on Eli's bedroom door. I wasn't sure what he'd do if he caught me and I definitely didn't want to find out.

There was only one key that appeared small enough that it would fit into the lock. I wasn't sure it would fit but after jiggling it, the key slipped into place.

My breaths hit me quickly as I turned the key and opened the small door. I raised the candle, illuminating the various amber bottles, some with pharmacy labels, some with other labels. The one that caught my eye had a warning label.

I took it out and almost dropped it when I saw the word printed under the warning. Arsenic.

I shoved it back into the metal box and closed the door. My fingers fumbled the keys as I tried to lock the box.

"Come on," I whispered. Sucking in a breath when I felt the key turn.

I raced back to the coat hook and shoved Eli's keys back into his coat pocket. Once I was back in the bedroom, I closed the door and grabbed our things, setting them into a pile.

"Shit!" I said remembering that Eli had taken our guns.

I'd get Leah ready, then we'd get the guns. The important thing was to get far away from Eli before he woke.

I didn't know how I was going to help Leah. After seeing the poison in the kitchen, I instantly knew that Leah wasn't suffering from an infection. She'd been poisoned. And so had I. I hoped to hell that once we got away, things would improve.

"Leah," I said shaking her lightly. "You need to wake up."

She didn't respond. Her body moved with my shaking from side to side.

I reached around her, helping her sit up. Her body was heavy even though she was so thin.

In the dim light, I could see more hair had fallen out onto her pillow. I chewed my lip and shook her again.

"Leah. Wake up," I said.

She started to fall forward but I caught her. I straightened her as best as I could but it was like posing a doll. She wouldn't stay in place.

I touched her forehead and gasped. The coldness of her body was shocking. I lowered her back down on the bed carefully and tried to wake her again.

"Leah, please," I begged. "I need you to wake up."

I got off the bed and grabbed the candle from the

nightstand. The muscles in her face were slack and there was a blueish tinge to her lips.

"Oh, God. Leah, no," I said sniffing hard as a tear stung my eye.

I grabbed her wrist but I couldn't find a pulse. I probably couldn't have found a pulse either way.

I set down the candle and dropped my head down to her chest. Nothing.

I pressed down repeatedly, trying to pump the life back into her but her body just flopped lifelessly on the bed.

I had no idea how much time had passed before I stood and started to pace. My hand shook as I ran them through my hair over and over again.

"What should I do?" I asked if Leah would somehow be able to tell me.

I couldn't leave her like this but if I stayed, I'd certainly die. Eli would suspect something when I refused to eat and drink his food.

How could I have been so stupid? I sat down next to Leah again, holding my hand next to her nose, desperately hoping to feel her breath.

I couldn't do this on my own.

She would want me to go. Eva was still in the corner of the room laughing but Leah was in the other corner yelling at me to get the hell out of there.

I wrapped my arms around Leah's lifeless body,

hugging her tightly to me. Her arms hung down heavily at her sides. "I love you. I love you so damn much. I am so sorry I failed you."

The bedroom door flung open. Eli was standing there with his arms crossed.

"What the hell is going on in here?" he boomed.

"I'm sorry," I said not realizing that I had been loud. "She... she didn't make it."

"Oh," Eli said. He stared at me and started shifting his weight from one foot to the other. "Why are your bags here?"

I rubbed my palms against the sides of my legs. "I was looking for something."

"At what point do you want me to remind you of the cameras?" Eli asked.

Oh, shit. He'd mentioned that he'd seen us coming. The cameras hadn't only been outside, he'd had them placed inside the house too.

"I know what you found," Eli said.

"Why? Why did you do this?" I asked. If there was one thing I wanted to know before he killed me, it was why.

"You damn no-good kids were just going to steal from me, just like all the ones before," Eli said. "I had to do everything I could to protect myself, my things, and now, my niece too."

I shook my head. "So, you killed her? And tried to

kill me? We would have just left. We didn't want your things. The only reason we came here was because Heather wanted us to."

"I would have been a fool to sit here and do nothing, waiting for the day you tried to harm or deceive us," Eli said.

"You're crazy," I said.

"What's going on, Uncle Eli?" Heather said stepping up beside him.

I huffed. "I'll tell you what's going on. Your uncle killed my girlfriend."

Heather instantly started shaking her head. "That doesn't make any sense."

"I'm pretty sure he's done it before, too," I said jerking my thumb toward the window. "There are gravestones not far from the side of the house."

Eli's lips pressed together. He didn't even try to deny it.

"Uncle Eli, is this true?" Heather asked.

"I'm going to protect you. Your parents weren't able to but I will," Eli said.

She stepped up to him and hit him in the side of the arm. "Did you do this?"

Eli pulled his arm back and smacked her so hard he flung her into the wall. Heather lost her balance and fell to the floor, her legs tangled underneath her.

I had to figure out a way to get out of the cabin. Eli

was blocking the door, I didn't have my gun, and Heather was sobbing on the floor.

Heather covered her ears and squeezed her eyes shut. "They helped me, Uncle Eli! How could you do this? They're not bad! You are! You're terrible, just like my dad said!"

"Shut up!" Eli bellowed so loudly, the walls shook.

I sucked in a breath and charged forward.

STEVIE

In the morning, they brought us bowls of mush. Oatmeal maybe. I was given half the amount of everyone else but I didn't care.

The beating they'd given me hadn't been enough for their sadistic souls. They needed to starve me too.

I didn't eat it. I didn't want it anyway.

"Stevie," Melinda said sitting down next to me at the window. I stared out, wondering what Gage and Shawn were doing. Were they taking care of Jake? Was he even alive? "If you really have something waiting out there, you can't do this."

"I'm not doing anything," I muttered before resting my chin on my fist.

"That's exactly what I'm saying," she said. "You need to get back there to them. Whoever is there is probably waiting for you, right?"

I pressed my lips together so they wouldn't tremble.

"A boyfriend, maybe? A husband? Maybe a child?" she asked.

I swallowed hard. My mouth was dryer than the desert. I couldn't speak but I gave her a nod.

"Boyfriend?" she asked.

My head bobbed once.

There was a quick glimmer in Melinda's eyes that quickly faded. "Are there other boys there?"

"Yes."

"Well, then, we can't give up. You can't give up," Melinda said. "I'll help you. We'll all help you."

I frowned. "You don't get it, do you?"

"It's you that doesn't get it." Melinda scowled.

"I'm not going to risk anything happening to anyone else. There has been enough death," I said.

"They'll be letting me out later to help with dinner," Melinda said looking at the others. "I can easily get to the knives."

"And I can get the keys to get us out of here," Ida said. "That bastard will come for me tonight. I'll get him to drink a lot before he has his way with me. I've never been brave enough to steal the keys before but knowing there is something else out there helps. I'm willing to risk anything to get out of this place."

I shook my head. "This is a terrible idea. I don't want anyone to get hurt."

"I'll get weapons," Melinda said.

"I'll get the keys," I said.

They were making plans. I wished I had confidence that we'd be okay. That we could pull this off and no one would get hurt.

Tami twisted her fingers. "What can I do to help?"

"When we get out, you and Abigail run through town, carefully switching off the lanterns," Melinda said tapping her finger on her chin. "I think this could really work."

"Or it could fail horribly," I said. "We could all end up dead."

"We're already dead here," Ida mumbled.

Melinda's brow wrinkled. "What happened to that girl they threw in here? The one with the fighting spirit. The one that wasn't afraid of these wretched men."

"They killed her," I said turning toward the window. I sniffed and swallowed back the lump in the back of my throat. "She died with Lydia."

"No," Melinda said placing her hand on my cheek. She placed her fingers on my chin and turned me to face her. "They didn't. I still see her in there. Fight to get her back. We need her. Do it for us. Do it for Lydia. Do it for the people you have back at your place."

My shoulders slumped. It felt as though the muscles in my body had all been sliced in half and there wasn't anything to hold me together.

"Please," Abigail said. "Help us. We need you. We won't ever get a chance like this again."

Tami nodded enthusiastically.

"You really want to do this? It's dangerous," I said.

"Yes," Melinda said. "And the other women will want to be there with us. All of us together, we can get out of here. There are more of us than there are of them."

I shook my head. "It's possible that not everyone will make it out."

"We need to try, right ladies?" Melinda said flapping her hands, urging the others to agree.

"Yes!" Tami said.

Abigail's head bobbed.

Ida looked at her nails and then at me. "If it means I'll never have to lay in that dreadful man's sweat-stained bed again, I'm one hundred percent in."

Something in my core shifted. All the pieces inside me started to come back together. I thought of Shawn, and Gage, and the others too, as my outer shell toughened. They wouldn't want me to stop fighting. Ever.

"Okay," I said letting the smile curl my lips. "Let's do it."

Just as Melinda said they would, men came for her

to help prepare dinner. Hours later, an armed, hideous, gray-haired man with rotten teeth came for Ida.

They were out of the house and there wasn't anything I could do but wait. Ida would come with the keys to let us out... to let us all out from each of the houses and Melinda would take us to the kitchen to arm ourselves with knives. Tami and Abigail would sneak around, turning off the lights.

We'd all escape. It almost seemed too easy but I knew it wouldn't be.

I paced as my stomach twisted. I didn't want anything to go wrong.

The only reason the women hadn't tried sooner was because they had nowhere to go. They'd believed all that was out there for them was death and while they didn't like being prisoners, none of them were ready to die.

It had been night for hours and there was no word from either Ida or Melinda. I could hear my heart pounding in my head.

"Something went wrong," I said.

"Don't say that," Abigail said puffing out her lip.

I turned at the sound of someone at the door. There was a heavy thud followed by a key being inserted into the lock.

Ida stepped inside, holding her hands out to the side. There was blood staining her clothes.

"I hated him, you know?" I Ida said as her breaths shook her. "I don't know why I feel bad about it."

"He was a bad person for everything he did to you," I said.

"He really was," Tami said from behind me. "It wasn't just you, he was hurting a lot of us and you saved us from him."

Ida's lip quivered as she stared at Tami. "I... I didn't know he was doing this to you."

"It's okay," Tami said. She squinted as she looked out of the door. "Where's Melinda?"

"Still in the kitchen," Ida said.

"What should we do?" Tami asked.

I sucked in a breath. "You and Abigail go to Melinda and get your weapons. Ida and I will let the others out and meet you there."

"Okay," Tami said giving Ida a quick hug. "See you soon."

Ida handed me the keys. Her hands were still shaking. "Take these."

The light outside our door went out. Lightning flashed in the distance.

"Let's go," I said.

Ida led me from house to house. At each stop, she quickly explained what was happening to everyone inside. All of the women followed us without asking many questions.

She told them they could choose to stay but there was something better out there. A place where they wouldn't be held captive. Where they wouldn't have to do things against their will.

They followed us to the kitchen. It was impossible to keep them quiet but we tried.

The storm was growing closer. Every few minutes, a lightning strike would flash and light us.

"Shh!" I said vigorously tapping my finger to my lips. "I heard something."

The men were shouting. They knew we had escaped.

"They're coming!" someone said. There was a touch of excitement in her voice.

I moved to the front of the line and got a knife from Melinda. She smiled and handed me a cleaver. The edge glistened with a flicker of lightning.

"Saved this one just for you," Melinda said.

I patted her shoulder. "Make sure you grab one for yourself. They're coming."

"Hurry, ladies!" Melinda called. "It's payback time!"

The woman hooted and hollered. They were ready. They were greater warriors than I would ever be.

I wasn't fit to lead them but I didn't have a choice. It was time.

I ran to the front of the group. We had to run to the south, guided only by the flashes of lightning.

"Ready to fight?" I asked, my voice falling with the rain. I cleared my throat and raised my voice. "Are you ready to fight?"

The women roared.

Lightning flashed again. I saw Ida standing at the front with a steak knife in hand. Tami and Abigail were in the middle of the group, both smiling at me.

I looked away, hoping they would be okay. I turned and came face to face with the barrel of a gun.

"What do you think you're doing?" the man asked.

"We're leaving," the woman behind me said. She stepped forward and jammed her blade into the man's side.

He grunted and leaned forward. The woman easily pulled the gun from him and laughed.

A few others joined in. The sound of the gunshot instantly stopped the laughter. There was a scream from my left.

My eyes darted around, trying to find where the gunman was. There was another gunshot. And then another.

"Run!" I said and they followed me.

I smacked into a man. My hand moved quickly, hacking him once in the neck and then again in the arm as he was falling to the ground.

Lightning struck nearby and the earth shook. I looked over my shoulder to see the group of women had thinned.

My eyes locked with Tami's and then Ida's. I could see they were anxious for me to keep everyone moving even while the shots rang out.

Women screamed with each pop. There were howls and moans. It was only a matter of time before we were all on the ground... dead.

There was another shot. It was close. Too close.

Ida was on the ground. Her hands around her stomach.

I cried out my frustration. I didn't want anyone to get hurt and here we were... fighting... dying.

I sucked in a breath and dropped to my knees. "Nooo!"

JOSS

My eyes darted around the floor. I spotted one of the guns and picked it up.

"Stay with Jenna," I called as I pushed my way through the door.

The ringing of the bell above was like sharp needles pushing into my brain. I scanned the area as tears rolled down my cheeks.

I was terrified. Not because of what might happen to me but because of what could happen to Cal.

"Where are you!" I screamed.

Why did they want a baby? Was it just to raise him in their strange cult? Maybe it was because he was a boy... but they wouldn't have known that just by seeing him. At least, I didn't think they would have.

I gasped when I spotted Ned. He'd gotten further away than I had expected.

I raised the gun but I couldn't shoot. Even if I would have, I likely would have missed. I couldn't risk anything happening to Cal.

My feet splashed through the mud. I ran so fast it felt like I was flying... or maybe like I was being carried. Was it possible that Robby and Caleb were with me? Helping me. Nah. Maybe?

The rain hitting my cheeks was like little razor blades slashing my cheeks. It stung but I didn't care. I kept going.

I came upon them and Ned stopped. He must have heard me behind him.

"Let him go," Ned said. "I'm not giving him up."

"Why? What are you going to do with a baby?" I asked.

"I need to go back with something, or they'll kill me," Ned said. "I can't fail."

I shook my head. "You can't steal someone's baby."

"Then you come back with me," Ned said.

"A trade?" I asked.

"Sure," Ned said. "You and the other girl. Then the girl can have her baby back."

My stomach turned. "I can't make that deal for someone else but I'll go with you if you give him up."

"He's more valuable than you are," Ned said. "My boss will wonder how we've lost three men for one woman. But the baby, we can shape and mold. We can raise him to be like us."

Ned stared at me for a long moment. He tightened his grip on the gun.

"Never mind," Ned said. "The deal is off."

I jerked my hand up and shot him in the leg only seconds before he pulled the trigger. Ned fell to his knees and his arm jerked upward as he cried out in pain. The bullet ripped through the air somewhere above my head.

Blood gushed out of the hole I'd made in his leg. Ned let Cal roll out of his arm and into the mud. He pressed the hand that had been holding Cal against the wound.

Without the baby in his arm, I knew I had to do it. I had to kill him.

I held my breath and fired again. The sound was deafening. My ears were ringing.

Ned stared at me. He didn't blink. It looked like he'd been frozen.

After what felt like an eternity, he flopped forward. His face pressed down into the mud.

I kept my gun aimed at him as I dashed forward and picked Cal off the ground. There was a little frown on his face. He was on the verge of bursting into tears.

"It's okay," I whispered. "It's over now. We'll go back to Mommy, okay?"

I took a step back but something grabbed my ankle. I looked down at the fingers digging into me.

The wide eyes of Ned's mud-covered face stared at me. I shot him again and his entire body shook. His limp hand fell away and I ran back to the gas station just as fast as I had run from it to get Cal.

Again, it felt like I was being carried.

When I returned, Jenna was awake. She whimpered at the sight of us coming in through the door.

Jenna grabbed Cal and pressed him to her chest. She wrapped an arm around me.

"Are you okay?" Jenna asked.

"I'm fine." I pulled back looking at her head. "How about you?"

"Just a bump. How will I ever be able to thank you?" she said between her tears.

I hugged her back. "I'm just glad we're all back together."

I waved Allie to us and she huddled in. Her breaths were quick and her eyes stayed on the bodies but she was okay.

"Let's get out of here," I said.

Jenna quickly cleaned Cal with the baby wipes. We packed a few things, took the guns, and left.

As we walked, I couldn't stop thinking about what I'd done. I'd saved Cal. I ran toward danger instead of hiding from it.

Of course, it wasn't like I had a choice. I'd made a promise to Cal. I was going to keep him safe no matter what.

My strength had surprised me. Maybe we would be okay. Maybe I was more of a fighter than I gave myself credit for.

After all, I was still here. I was still going. I was pretty sure that wherever Robby and Caleb were, they were looking at me with smiles on their faces. I wasn't just a follower... I was a fighter too.

Clover came up next to me and meowed. I picked her up and hugged her.

"I'm not a very good pet parent, am I?" I asked pressing my cheek to the top of her head.

I looked at her and smiled. Her eyes narrowed but it looked like she was smiling back. Clover no doubt thought she was the one taking care of me.

———

I wasn't sure how many days had gone by before we saw the grouping of houses come into view. It was like a small town with nothing but small roads, houses, and flooded fields.

"What kind of place is this?" Jenna asked.

"A ranch?" Allie questioned.

"Should we go another way?" Jenna wondered as she looked around nervously.

My mouth dried. I swallowed hard as I turned toward Allie. "This isn't where you were held, is it?"

"No," Allie said. "Nothing like this. I was in a town. An actual town."

"That doesn't mean those guys aren't here," Jenna said.

A young man stepped out onto the porch of one of the houses. He wasn't wearing a bulletproof vest but that didn't mean much.

He said something to someone in the house. I couldn't hear him but I could see his mouth moving.

"We should go," Jenna said.

The young man nodded to the other person and walked over to us. He held up his hands as he approached.

"Hey," he said. "Are you guys okay?"

"Yes," Jenna said holding Cal tighter.

"Where are you coming from?" he asked.

I sighed. "Nowhere, really."

"You all look tired," he said sticking out his hand. "I'm Shawn. We've got a lot of space here if you want a place to stay."

"That's not necessary," I said crossing my arms.

Shawn took a step back. "We're good people here. I know that might be hard for you to believe but it's true.

There are other people here who took their time adjusting to our more normal way of life."

"What do you make people do?" Allie asked.

"Nothing." Shawn shrugged. "Most people do choose to pitch it once they adjust."

I stared at him. There seemed to be nothing but sincerity in his eyes. Of course, that could be faked.

"How about you come inside and meet some of the others," Shawn said with a smile. "You can sit down, have something to eat and drink. Your cat looks like she'd like to dry off. You all do."

"I'm not sure," I said looking at Jenna first then at Allie.

"Okay," Shawn said. He pointed at one of the houses. "I understand. That house is empty. Go inside, think it over. I'll bring some food over and set it on the porch. If you want to stay, come ask for me. And if you want to go, just walk away. Of course, I, rather we, hope you'll stay."

We agreed to stay in the empty house. Temporarily.

I stared out the window, watching everyone move around the area. There were a lot of people. They seemed friendly. Normal.

Everyone left us alone. Even when the food was dropped off, a young girl knocked on the door and walked off.

Jenna and Allie chowed down ravenously. I grazed on the items they'd brought to us but didn't want to leave my post at the window.

I clutched the ring from Robby and waited... and watched. It was like I was desperate for a sign. Should we stay? Or should we go?

It was a short while later they brought over a closed cardboard box. Jenna opened it carefully and started crying when she saw the cat food, diapers, and clothing, not just for the baby, but for all of us.

"Note says they guessed at the sizes," Jenna said setting it aside. "If we need something else to just let them know. Did we die?"

"I don't think this is heaven," Allie said. "But it seems pretty good."

"So, you think we should stay?" I asked.

Jenna shrugged but the smile on her face was giving away her answer. "We can give it a shot, right? I think if they were still with us, they'd tell us to stay."

I looked down at the ring. The light outside caught it and there was a flash of a sparkle.

A sign?

Maybe.

I always thought I needed someone to take care of me but after what happened, I knew that was no longer true. I could take care of myself and look out for Jenna, Cal, and Allie too.

There was no point in venturing out into the unknown when we had a shelter. I wish there was a way to know if we were safe from the other people around. They weren't the men in the vests and that was a plus.

The men and women around worked together. They didn't look unhappy or as though they were prisoners.

If it was the wrong choice, we'd figure it out. But something told me... it wasn't. Staying would be the right thing for us. The safe thing for us.

Cal needed a roof over his head. He needed a home—a place where we could take care of him.

There was a chance we'd found it... and I couldn't let us walk away from that.

"Okay," I said. "You're probably right."

I pulled in a breath and pushed my shoulders back. After everything I'd been through, I felt different. Stronger.

I covered my mouth, so no one saw my smile. I barely recognized myself but that was a good thing.

"I'll go talk to them," I said. "See what this is all about."

"Eat some more. You barely touched your food," Jenna said. "It can wait."

I nodded and turned away from the window. I sat

down on the floor and looked through the items we were given.

It seemed as though we were going to be okay. We'd made it to safety together, and in one piece.

I started laughing. Robby and Caleb would never have believed it. Or maybe they knew what I was capable of all along.

ADAM

Rage fueled me. I threw my fist into Eli's gut as hard as I could. My knuckle cracked as it slammed into a rib.

"Oof!" Eli grunted as he tipped forward.

I shook my hand. The pain radiated down my forearm, stopping at my elbow.

Eli was at least twice my size. It felt like I was in a battle with a yeti. He'd been living well since everything happened and I'd struggled. Not to mention having likely been poisoned over the last couple of days.

It was like I was staring into the darkness of Death's face and surprisingly, I wasn't as frightened as I thought I'd be. I knew the day would come and now that it had, I was ready to fight.

Leah wouldn't want me to give up. She would want me to give it everything I had.

Eli grabbed the front of my shirt and lifted me of the ground. My hands wrapped tightly around his arm, twisting the skin. I dangled, my toes barely touching the wooden floor.

He growled as he slammed his fist into the side of my face. My head jerked to the side as my mouth filled with the taste of pennies.

The room blurred. Eli tossed me to the side like a bag of trash.

"Stop it, Uncle!" Heather screamed as she leaped onto his back and pounded him with her closed hands. "Don't do this! Please!"

Eli moved sharply from side to side like a bull bucking off its rider. Heather dug her fingers into back deeper, refusing to be flung off him.

I scrambled to my feet and punched him in the nose. He twisted at the unexpected blow. Blood gushed out of one nostril, splattering with his sharp, furious exhale.

"That's it!" Eli spat.

He roared as I ducked under his arm and dashed toward the kitchen. Eli was slow with Heather on his back and thanks to my nosiness, I knew exactly where he stored the long, sharp kitchen knives.

I pulled open the drawer, grabbing the two longest

knives I spotted. With a blade in each hand, I sprinted toward Eli.

Releasing an agonizing, revenge filled cry, I jabbed the knife into his right shoulder. Heather slid off and took several steps back. She was frozen in place, watching me with wide, round eyes.

I grunted as I raised my left hand.

"No!" Heather shouted. "Please don't. He's all I have left."

I ignored her, slicing the side of Eli's arm. He dropped to his knees.

"Adam! Please," Heather begged.

"He killed her," I said pointing the tip of the knife at Eli's face.

"He's the only family I have left," Heather said.

Eli dropped to his knees. He didn't beg for his life in words but I could see him pleading for me not to kill him in his eyes.

I shook my head. "What will stop him from doing the same to you?"

"He won't," Heather said.

"Come with me," I said.

She shook her head.

"You're sure?"

"Sorry, Adam," she said. "Thank you for every-thing you've done for me."

I looked at her for a second and gave her a nod. "Okay. But I have to do just one more thing."

She narrowed her eyes.

With every last bit of energy I had left in my body, which wasn't as much as I would have liked, I kicked Eli in the face. His eyes rolled back and he dropped to the floor.

"Why did you do that?" Heather squeaked.

"I need to get my things and get out of here," I said. "There's no way he would have let me go."

"He's not dead, is he?" Heather asked.

I gave her a loose shrug. Honestly, I didn't care if he was.

"I don't think so," I said. "You'll need to treat those wounds."

Heather crossed her arms and met my eyes. "Get your things."

I placed my hand on her shoulder and gave her a quick squeeze before I grabbed my bags from the bedroom. I couldn't stop my eyes from darting over to Leah, who was in the same position I'd left her in.

"I'm sorry," I whispered.

My shoulders dropped and I left the room, wishing I would have told her more often how much she meant to me. And how she had made me a better person.

I ran to the bunker and grabbed our two guns. Without another word, I left.

I'd run from the house, through the trees, through the rain without stopping. At first, it was so dark I hadn't been able to travel quickly but it wasn't long before gray morning light lit the sky, helping me see my way.

It was hard to keep moving with my heart shattered. Several times, I considered turning the gun on myself so that I could join her.

Of course, I couldn't. Either I was a coward or I knew how pissed she'd be if I did something like that.

I kept going south.

The days passed. I didn't count them. I didn't care to. All I did was wait for something to go wrong or for Eli to come after me and finish what he'd started.

I was lucky that I was able to get the poison, or at least most of it, out of my system. The stuff in my backpack diminished quickly. I hadn't found much but I was somehow surviving.

When the houses came into view, my first thought was to turn and run as fast as I could. But I had to check for food and supplies. I'd be quick... and careful.

As I cautiously approached the first house. I saw a young girl playing in a mud puddle at the furthest house.

She stopped jumping when she saw me. The little girl smiled and waved.

Seconds later, a woman came out of one of the houses across the street. She looked over at the girl and hesitated. The woman turned slowly and saw me standing there.

My hand moved to my waistband. I was ready to fight.

But then something happened. I'd seen the woman before, although I couldn't remember where I'd seen her.

Her eyes narrowed as she took small steps toward me. She wrapped her arms around her middle as the rain drenched her dry clothes.

"Do you need help?" she asked stopping more than fifteen feet away from me. Her nose wrinkled. "I know you from somewhere. Or maybe you just have one of those faces."

"Then you have one of those faces too," I said.

"Are you armed?" she asked.

I nodded. "For safety reasons."

"Oh, trust me," she said with a smile. "I understand. But please, don't shoot me. I'm not armed."

"Then don't do anything stupid," I said.

She laughed. "I've done plenty stupid."

It hit me like getting slapped in the face. She was the girl who supposedly had been stealing supplies from the resort.

"I do know you," I said.

She cocked her head to the side.

"I was at the resort. One of the people I worked for caught you and your partner stealing," I explained. "Your friend didn't make it."

A grin grew on her face. "Holy crap! Yeah, that's it. You... you helped me. I'd be dead if... that guy was definitely not my friend."

"The guy I was with at the time wasn't my friend either," I said matching her smile. "It's crazy seeing you here. That was a long time ago."

"It sure was," she said bravely walking toward me. She stretched out her hand. "I'm Joss."

"Adam," I said.

She stared at me for a long moment. "It's really nice to meet you."

"You too," I said.

"Look, if you're in need of a place to stay, this is it," Joss said. "I know you probably don't believe me but I'm finally sleeping through the night again."

I wiped the rain off the back of my neck. "I have no idea what that's like."

"I'll introduce you around," Joss said.

I didn't move. "I don't know if I can do this again."

"Can I ask what happened?"

"You can ask but I'm not ready. It's hell out there," I said but she already knew that. "The people from the resort started a war with your people."

Joss looked to the side and nodded. "The town I was in was destroyed. At least, I'm pretty sure it was. There were fires and explosions."

"But you survived?"

"I ran away," Joss said. She offered me a tight-lipped smile. "Now I'm here and I really hope this is it. There isn't anywhere else for us to go."

"Are there a lot of people here?" I asked.

Joss nodded. "And it's nothing like anywhere else I've been. Everyone wants the same thing."

"Sure thing," I huffed. "I'll believe it when I see it."

"So, you'll stay?" Joss asked hopefully.

I shrugged. "Maybe."

She jerked her head and I followed her.

I met the people in charge. There were so many smiling faces that it made me a bit nervous. They gave me food and water and a place to sleep in the same house as Joss.

The first night, I didn't sleep much, but I slept more and more with each passing night. I felt quicker. Healthier.

I missed Leah and I wished she would have been able to see the compound. If she was looking down on me, she was smiling and cheering, happy I'd made it.

I could almost hear her telling me that I won. I beat Eva.

Of course, I'd trade everything just to have Leah

back but it was because of her I'd keep going. There was no doubt in my mind that it would be what she'd want.

I knew a day wouldn't go by that I wouldn't think of her. She was my everything. When we'd meet again, she be so damn proud of me. That would keep me going.

I made it on my own. Money didn't get me here, nor didn't power or connections. I found my way all on my own.

I'd be okay. I would find a way to be okay.

STEVIE

Ida grabbed my hand. "You need to get up and keep going. The women are fighting. They're strong. The gunshots are slowing. You're winning. Don't give up now. You need to get as many of them as you can out of here. Do you understand me?"

Lightning flashed again, stopping me from responding. I could see all the people lying on the ground but what I couldn't tell was who they were.

Some of the women behind me now had guns. I hadn't realized they'd even taken them. It wasn't just the men shooting... we'd been shooting back.

"Go, Stevie," Ida said before closing her eyes. "Get them out. You... can... do... it."

I squeezed her hand. "I will."

I stood. The longer we stayed in one spot, the more

likely it was we'd lose more women. I didn't want to lose anyone else.

"Let's move!" I shouted.

We ran. The flashes of light guided us and with each step, the sounds of gunshots faded until there were none.

With the next flash of light, I looked back. The houses were far behind us. We had made it out of town.

Hope filled me. A smile teased my lips but I pushed it away. It was a long way back to the compound. I could smile when I got everyone there safely.

I would see Shawn again. I would see Gage again. And I couldn't wait.

We walked through the night. The storm faded before the light turned to a bright gray.

Our pace had slowed but we figured out long ago that no one was behind us. More of the women had made it than I had initially thought.

Melinda, Tami, and Abigail were all there. Smiling and hugging. They didn't even care that it was raining down on us.

"Thank you, Stevie," Melinda said stepping up beside me.

"It was all you guys," I said smiling back at her.

"We couldn't have done it without you, Stevie," Tami said placing her hand on my shoulder.

I shook my head. "Yes, you could have!"

"We wouldn't have known where to go," Tami said with a laugh. "Seriously, though, we owe you."

"Oh, shit," Melinda said her eyes narrowed.

I turned sharply, meeting her eyes. "What is it?"

"People," Melinda said. All joy washed away from her. "What should we do?"

"We can fight!" Tami said, her adrenaline still pumping.

"Maybe," I said.

There was something about the group of people coming toward us that was different. I froze. A shiver ran up my spine and my throat filled with a pocket of air.

Heat seared my eyes and I covered my mouth with my shaking hand.

"Are you okay?" Melinda asked.

"I know them," I said between my tears. "I know them."

"Your people?" Melinda asked.

My head bobbed. I tried to get to my feet but I was too weak. It was like I was fully feeling the beating I had taken.

"Hey!" Melinda shouted as she waved. "Stevie needs you!"

I could see Shawn between the legs of the women surrounding me. He dropped something and started running.

"Stevie!" he called as he pushed through the group.

Our eyes met and he dropped down in the mud next to me. He wrapped his arms around me and squeezed.

"Ow," I said wincing. The pain didn't stop me from squeezing him back.

"Jesus, Stevie," he said placing his hands on my face. "What happened to you?"

I swallowed hard. "They didn't like me."

"Crazy talk," Shawn said. "Everyone loves you. They all came out here to get you back."

I bit my lip as Shawn stared into my eyes.

He kept his voice low. "I was worried I'd never see you again."

Shawn pulled me close and kissed me. I kissed him back as if filling myself with oxygen. I hadn't realized how hard it was to breathe without Shawn at my side.

"I love you," I said.

"Oh, God," Shawn said. "You have no idea how amazing that is to hear right now. I love you too."

Gage dropped down beside me, shoving Shawn to the side. "Dammit, Stevie. You can't do shit like that."

Shawn held out his hands at his sides. "Seriously?"

I laughed as Gage hugged me. "I missed you too,"

"Are you okay?" Gage asked. "You look like shit."

"Thanks," I said. "Help me up."

Gage and Shawn each took an arm. Shawn wrapped an arm around me and I leaned on him.

"Everyone, this is everyone," I said.

The women were apprehensive but they smiled and nodded at my friends. I noticed Kieran and Jake weren't there but that wasn't surprising.

"Is Jake okay?" I asked.

"He's hanging in there," Gage said.

"Good," I said reaching into my pocket. "Because I got this."

A smile stretched across Shawn's face. "You're freaking amazing."

"Before we go back and give him the good news, we have to go back to the town and finish what you started," Gage said. "For our own safety."

"I'll lead everyone back," Ella said. "You should come with us, Stevie."

Shawn's head was bobbing in agreement but I shook mine.

"I'm fine. I'll be able to help," I said.

The walk back went quicker during the day than it had at night. It wasn't long before I saw the bodies scattered on the ground.

Men... and women.

So many lives were lost.

I showed everyone around. If any of the men had survived, they were long gone... except for one.

Zachary stood there in the doorway of his house. He had no intention of running. I could also tell that he hadn't joined in the fight.

"Who's this guy?" Shawn asked.

"The one that was in charge," I said.

"Are you happy?" Zachary shouted as he pounded his fists on the doorframe. "Is this what you wanted?"

It stunned me that I wasn't more afraid of the man who had ordered my beating. The man that sat there and watched as if it were entertainment.

"Me?" I asked with a laugh. "I wasn't the one keeping people locked up."

We stopped on the sidewalk in front of his house. Gage had been on my right but he took a step ahead of Shawn and me, ready to confront Zachary. Nearly my entire group of people stood bravely behind us.

"This is far from over. I will rebuild," Zachary said with a smirk as he waved his pistol at us. He didn't care that he was outnumbered.

"Oh, I don't think so," Gage said raising up his gun. "This couldn't be more over."

Zachary took several steps toward us. Rain poured down on him, plastering his hair to his forehead.

"I won't go out alone," Zachary said holding my gaze.

He raised his arms up at his sides, palms up toward the sky. His hands were nearly up to shoulder height when a gunshot from my left shook me.

My breath was stuck in my throat. I turned to Shawn, who was still holding his gun up as if he wasn't sure he was finished.

"He deserved it," Shawn said staring at Zachary's body. His breaths hit him hard. It seemed as though he had gone somewhere else.

I placed my hand on the gun and eased it down. I looked into Shawn's eyes, trying to bring him back.

"He did," I said.

Shawn blinked several times before handing the gun to Noah. He wrapped his arms around me.

"Let's go home," Shawn said.

I exhaled. "Yeah, let's go home."

Most of us headed south. Gage and some of the others did a quick sweep of the area before catching up.

Everyone welcomed me back and told me how much they missed me. I told them all how much I had missed them too.

I couldn't wait to get back home. And I was glad we no longer had to worry about the people in the town.

Once we finally reached the compound, some wanted to celebrate. I was far too tired and sore to do much of anything. Not to mention, I didn't feel like there was anything to celebrate. Too many lives had been lost.

There were still things for us to worry about. The wild animals were still out there, and there was still a possibility there were others out there.

Kieran patched me up while Gage made plans with the others to go back to the town to take what they could. I was exhausted and all I could think about was sleep.

I rested my head on Shawn's shoulder. Gage climbed up on the coffee table and held up his can of warm beer.

He flapped his hands and everyone quieted down.

"I just want to say how incredibly happy I am to have Stevie back," Gage said. Everyone cheered and my cheeks reddened. "We wouldn't have any of this if it wasn't for her. When the wave first hit in Florida, she saved me and every day since then, she's continued to save me."

"Get a room," Shawn shouted.

I smacked him and everyone laughed.

"Seriously, I wouldn't be here if it wasn't for her. A lot of us wouldn't be," Gage said.

The women from the town clapped. From across the room, Melinda tipped her invisible hat to me.

"She doesn't know how awesome she is," Gage

continued. "She has made this compound everything it is and it's only going to keep getting better."

"Oh, stop it," I said keeping my eyes down. The attention was making me sweat. "This place is what it is because of all of you. But I agree, it is going to keep getting better. Now, if you'll all go home so I can get some rest, I'd really appreciate it."

"Party next door!" someone shouted.

Melinda held her hands up. "Woo hoo!"

Tami and Abigail clapped enthusiastically. They were definitely going to enjoy their freedom.

I smiled and waved as everyone left. Shawn helped me up to bed. He kissed my forehead and I slept. And I slept.

———

Over the next few weeks, a handful of survivors made their way to us but it wasn't many. Those joining us had slowed down to the point where I didn't think we'd see anyone new again.

We'd helped so many people find a place to stay where they felt safe, or at least safe enough. The women from the town, a man who survived earthquakes in California, a young woman who'd lost the love of her life, and so many others were with us. They all had a story.

Everyone pitched in where they could. Our community worked together better than the world before The Reset.

Despite everything people had gone through, they seemed happy enough. Gage was happier ever since he started spending more time with Melinda.

And every morning, I thanked God I was with Shawn again. I rolled over and kissed his cheek, taking care not to wake him.

I got dressed and went downstairs before anyone else was up, like I always did. I liked to make sure everything was in order in the kitchen and that I'd know what we needed to work on each day.

Noah had been sitting in the chair at the window but I'd sent him to get some sleep. Even though we had other people stationed through the property to keep watch, we still liked to have someone watching the house.

Gage came down the stairs as I was picking up the gun. "Going somewhere?"

"Just getting some air," I replied.

"Mind if I join you?" Gage asked. "I need to keep an eye on you."

I raised a brow. "Was that Melinda I saw going up the stairs with you last night?"

"A gentleman doesn't speak of such things," Gage said fluttering his eyelashes.

I rolled my eyes and closed the door behind us. The air seemed a touch warmer than usual and the rain was just a drizzle.

I held out my cupped hand and let the rainfall into it. It was cool in my hand.

"This is the lightest the rain has been since this all happened," I said turning to Gage.

"Think I could run between the drops and stay dry?" Gage asked.

I shook my head. "Feel free to try it."

"I would but this is my favorite outfit."

"Sure," I said closing my eyes as I turned my head to the sky.

I took a step forward and let the rain wash down over me. It was like I wanted to show the rain that I wasn't afraid of it. That I wasn't going to let it hold power over me.

A smile curled my lips and I opened my eyes. Instead of letting out the massive breath I'd pulled in, I choked on it.

"Gage," I said grabbing his arm. I pointed up toward the sky. "Look!"

There was a break in the clouds. It was like giant hands were gently pulling apart the gray clouds that blanketed the sky.

"Holy shit!" Gage said looking around as if trying

to determine if he was awake. He ran his hands through his hair and laughed.

I could see the outline of them behind the thin clouds. It became brighter and brighter with each passing second. Before I knew it, the sun was too bright and I couldn't look at it.

"Look away," Gage said with a chuckle. His chest was rising and falling rapidly. "This can't be real, can it?"

"It seems real. It feels real."

"It won't stay like this," Gage said.

We both stood there, frozen in place, staring at the sky. We waited for the clouds to grow angry and cover the sun once again.

But it didn't happen.

I could feel the warmth of the sun on my skin, drying the rain droplets that were desperately trying to cling to me. A laugh erupted from deep within.

"Did we do it?" I asked in a soft voice. "Did we actually make it?"

"This is unbelievable," Gage said. He held out his hands as if he were trying to collect the sunlight, just in case it would vanish again.

The sun continued to grow and push away the rain clouds. I could see the brightest, bluest sky expanding above us.

I turned to Gage and hugged him. We had

somehow survived together.

"It's not going to last," Gage said but the smile on his face showed he hoped he was wrong.

The clouds were pulling apart for as far as I could see. It seemed as though it was finally... over.

"The sun is going to win," I said with so much positivity in my voice I barely recognized myself.

It was the first time in a long time, I thought we were actually going to be okay. With the sunlight, plants would grow again. The earth would be dry. We could build a fence to keep everything we had protected.

We would be safe.

It wasn't going to happen overnight but we'd be able to rebuild. I knew things wouldn't be how they'd been for a long time but at least with the sunlight, we could all have hope again that one day, we'd get there.

Maybe we'd get somewhere better.

We'd be warm.

We'd be dry.

We'd be the ones to start rebuilding. And I knew we'd be okay.

The others started to come out of the houses. Some smiled. Some wore expressions of surprise or shock.

I turned toward the house, barely able to contain myself. I opened the door and my voice burst from deep inside. "Shawn!"

BOOKS BY KELLEE L. GREENE

The Reset Series

Flood - Book 1

Sinking - Book 2

Drowned - Book 3

Swamp - Book 4

Torrent - Book 5

Striking - Book 6

What Remains Series

Sickness - Book 1

Outpost - Book 2

Infected - Book 3

Evasion - Book 4

Red Sky Series

Red Sky - Book 1

Blue Cloud - Book 2

Black Rain - Book 3

White Dust - Book 4

Indigo Ice - Book 5

Yellow Heat - Book 6

Ravaged Land Series (1)

Ravaged Land -Book 1

Finding Home - Book 2

Crashing Down - Book 3

Running Away - Book 4

Escaping Fear - Book 5

Fighting Back - Book 6

Ravaged Land: Divided Series (2)

The Last Disaster - Book 1

The Last Remnants - Book 2

The Last Struggle - Book 3

Ravaged Land: Eventuality Series (3)

The Wall - Book 1

The Outside - Book 2

Falling Darkness Series

Unholy - Book 1

Uprising - Book 2

Hunted - Book 3

The Island Series

The Island - Book 1

The Fight - Book 2

The Escape - Book 3

The Erased - Book 4

From Below Series

Creatures - Book 1

Desolation - Book 2

The Alien Invasion Series

The Landing - Book 1

The Aftermath - Book 2

Destined Realms Series

Destined - Book 1

MAILING LIST

Sign up for Kellee L. Greene's mailing list for new releases, sales, cover reveals and more!

Sign up: http://eepurl.com/bJLmrL

You can Find Kellee on Facebook:

www.facebook.com/kelleelgreene

ABOUT THE AUTHOR

Kellee L. Greene is a stay-at-home-mom to two super awesome and wonderfully sassy children. She loves to read, draw and spend time with her family when she's not writing. Writing and having people read her books has been a long time dream of hers and she's excited to write more. Her favorites genres are Fantasy and Sci-fi. Kellee lives in Wisconsin with her husband, two kids and two cats.

For more information:
www.kelleelgreene.com

facebook.com/kelleelgreene

twitter.com/kelleelgreene

bookbub.com/authors/kellee-l-greene

instagram.com/kelleelgreene